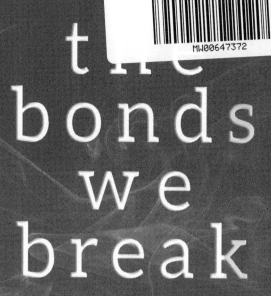

the bonds we break

BECCA STEELE

THE BONDS WE BREAK

THE FOUR - BOOK 5

BECCA STEELE

The Bonds We Break

Copyright © 2021 by Becca Steele

Anniversary edition Copyright © 2022 by Becca Steele

Editing by One Love Editing

Becca Steele

www.authorbeccasteele.com

AUTHOR'S NOTE

The author is British, and British English spellings and phrases are used throughout.

For Sue

Your heart knows the way. Run in that direction.

— *RUMI*

PROLOGUE

cassius

All the best love stories start with an epic blowjob.

Okay. Love might be stretching it a bit, unless it was possible to love someone's mouth. Especially when that mouth was talented as fuck and gave the best blowjobs I'd ever had the pleasure of receiving. And I'd received enough to make me a blowjob connoisseur.

Jessa De Witt, on her knees in front of me, those sexy, pouty red lips wrapped around my cock while her tongue flicked across the head, was the queen of sucking dick. Not only could she deep-throat better than anyone else, she loved it. A whole range of hot as fuck noises came from her throat as she sucked me down, sending vibrations all through my dick, while she tugged on my balls. My hands tangled in her long, glossy dark hair, and she let me fuck her face, opening her throat so I could thrust all the way in.

So. Good.

It felt like seconds before my balls were tightening and I was spilling my load down her throat.

After I'd put my dick away, I tugged her to her feet,

pulling her into me and sliding my mouth over hers in a messy kiss, tasting myself on her tongue.

She pulled her head back, staring at me, her green eyes glassy and unfocused. "Why do you like to taste yourself?"

I shrugged, a grin spreading across my face. "Because I taste good, babe."

She huffed out a disbelieving laugh. "You are so full of yourself, you know that?"

Avoiding the obvious reply, I flashed her another wide grin. "With good reason. Have you seen me?"

Shaking her head, she stepped backwards, but I stopped her by gripping her wrist.

"Where do you think you're going?"

"We're finished here, aren't we?" She glanced pointedly down in the direction of my cock.

Another tug and she was plastered against my body. "Do you want to ruin my reputation?" I put on a shocked voice, just so I could enjoy her resulting eye roll. "Let it never be said that Cassius Demetri Drummond doesn't satisfy his woman."

She glanced around us before returning her attention to me. "Firstly, in case you haven't noticed, we're in a roomful of people," she said, like I'd suddenly forgotten that we were in the middle of a party. Up against the wall in a darkish corner, but still, the party was going on all around us. Not that it bothered me—it wasn't the first time I'd had my cock sucked with other people around, and I wasn't the only one, either.

"Secondly," she continued, "I'm not your woman."

"Any other objections?" I gripped her sexy ass, palming it as I wedged my thigh between her legs.

"No..." The word was breathed out of her as she ground herself against my leg.

"Mmmm. That's it, baby. I know you don't care about these other people any more than I do." Dropping my lips to her neck, I bit down lightly. "And you know I'm not a one-woman man, just as you're not a one-man woman. We're only eighteen. Fuck being tied down—we have to spread the love. It's our duty as beautiful people."

"Where do you get these lines?" It sounded like she was caught between a laugh and a moan, and that wouldn't do. Snaking my hand in between us, I found her pussy bare and soaking, and I circled her clit.

When she whimpered, I smiled. Much better.

"Do you want my hand or my mouth?" I licked up her throat before blowing on her dampened skin, and she shuddered, grinding herself down on my leg.

"Any. Just hurry up," she panted.

"Mouth, then. I'm gonna make you come right in front of all these people." There wasn't really anyone paying attention to us, but I knew the thought of it would get her going more than anything else. It got me going, that was for fucking sure. My dick was already stirring again, even though I'd just come.

A low moan fell from her lips, her body rolling shame-lessly against mine. Taking hold of her hips, I stalled her movements, then dropped to my knees. There was a wet patch on my jeans where her pussy had ground against my leg, and my dick jumped.

Fucking hot.

With no underwear to bother with, I pushed up her dress, hooked her leg over my shoulder, and ate her out until she was sobbing out her orgasm over my face, the roomful of people forgotten.

Cassius rose to his feet, licking his lips with a slow, deliberate movement. I was distantly aware of the other people surrounding us, but at that moment, he had my attention. His dirty-blond hair was dishevelled, his blue eyes gleaming beneath his thick lashes as his mouth curved into a cocky grin.

"Good, huh?"

When my breathing was finally back to normal, I replied, "You know it was."

He dropped a kiss on my lips. "See ya later, babe." Before I could return his goodbye, he tugged me against him, his lips coming to my ear. "I fucking love your mouth."

Then he melted into the crowd and disappeared. When he'd gone, I made my way to the bathroom, straightening my dress and fixing my hair and makeup as best as I could. Blowing my reflection a kiss, I unlocked the bathroom door.

"There you are." Portia Thompson, my so-called best friend, strutted up to me, stunning as usual in a short black dress, her gorgeous red hair cascading down her back in loose waves. She stopped in front of me, looking me up and down. "Didn't we decide that mint green wasn't your colour?"

"I can pull it off." Tossing my hair over my shoulder, I gave her a look that dared her to disagree.

"If you say so." Her gaze flicked over me disdainfully. "Let's get a drink."

These caustic comments were the main reason I called her my so-called best friend, rather than my actual best friend. Sometimes I wondered if we even liked each other at all or if we just hung out together because it was what was expected of us, with our families being rich and influential.

We headed into the kitchen, and as usual, I ignored the whispers, the usual mix of envy and scathing comments. The queen bee's crown was heavy, but my position at the top was expected of me, and it wasn't like I could complain, anyway. I was one of the elite—a girl that other girls tried to emulate, with the attention of the hottest boys, always invited to the best parties. I worked hard, cultivating relationships that would be beneficial for my future, constantly maintaining the delicate balance between school and social life.

I thought I was untouchable, but I was wrong.

How easily it all came crashing down.

Cassius

Eighteen, maybe nineteen months ago. That was the last time I'd got my mouth on Jessa. Before things changed. Before Caiden caught her eye and their families tried to push them together. Before I met Winter Huntington and realised that maybe I was capable of catching feelings for someone.

By then, I'd been single for so long, I wasn't sure I could be any other way. Or even if I wanted to be, to be honest. My life was great; I had a steady stream of women, and the very occasional man, whenever I wanted. I had a group of best friends I'd lay down my life for, and my initial feelings

5

for Winter, whatever they were, had settled into a deep, pure friendship.

I didn't have one of those weird "feelings" like something was missing in my life.

Life was good, and I was happy.

I was the master of my own fucking destiny.

Everything was as it should be.

Until it wasn't.

1

jessa

The smell of petrol clung to my skin as I struggled against the ropes restraining me. I was angry, yes, but I was also afraid. More afraid than I'd ever been in my life.

Never show your hand.

My dad's words came back to me then, as the car took a sharp turn and I fell, my head smacking into the passenger-side door. The man in the driver's seat, the one with the scarred cheek, sour breath, and harsh eyes looked over at me and laughed, then said something in Russian that I didn't understand. I concentrated on breathing, in and out, slowly and steadily, even though my heart was pounding out of my chest.

Vivid images played through my mind. How had I let myself fall into this situation to begin with? I'd been in my flat, watching TV on my bed, when I'd received a text from Caiden Cavendish saying he needed to speak with me in person, asking me to come outside to give him a minute of my time. It was stupid of me to hope for anything—it was clear that he was in love with Winter Huntington, and

7

nothing and no one was going to come between them. But still, I went. Sheltering from the rain in the porch of the front door of the apartment building in my pyjama shorts set with a thin cardigan on top, I watched as a car pulled up, blinding me with its headlights.

I hadn't even had a chance to get away.

The man glanced over at me again, and then after flicking his gaze back to the road, he appeared to take a closer look, his oily gaze sliding over me, thick and slimy, sending pinpricks of disgust through my body. I'd had plenty of men look at me that way before, and I'd welcomed the attention, craved it even, but here, now, this was wrong.

So wrong.

His hand settled on my bare thigh. I jolted, and his fingers squeezed tighter. I sucked in a sharp breath as my gaze dragged down to his pale, thick fingers, heavy with rings, the tip of one finger missing.

I shuddered in revulsion as his blunt nails dug into my skin, flinging my head round almost on instinct and spitting in his face.

The car jerked, wheels spinning on the rain-slicked road. "*Suka!*" His incensed growl of rage gave me temporary satisfaction before his hand swung out, snapping my head back around with the force of the blow. Collapsing back into the car door again, I closed my eyes, holding myself still, breathing through the throbbing pain down the side of my face. At least his hand was gone now.

Without any warning, the car pulled to a sudden stop. The next thing I knew, my door was yanked open, and I would've fallen out of the side if there hadn't been a body already there, dragging me out. Kicking out, I screamed and shouted against my captor as the sound of another car stopping behind us filled me with wild hope.

A hope that was extinguished the next second as a rough hand clamped over my mouth. Desperately blinking my eyes against the driving rain, I watched as two figures spoke in harsh, guttural tones before the man who had taken me got right up in my face and spat. "*Suka*," he snarled, and I lashed out again, landing a kick to his shin that probably hurt my bare toes more than him.

The man now holding me laughed, removing his hand from my mouth, and I sucked in a deep breath before screaming at the top of my lungs. My scream was abruptly cut off when a heavy, rough fabric came down over my mouth, gagging me and preventing me from speaking. It was only then that I realised that my whole body was shivering, my clothing soaked through from the downpour.

More words were exchanged as I slumped back against the man holding me, my body suddenly weak and helpless. Then there were words spoken in my ear, this time in heavily accented English.

"Pretty little whore." His hand gripped my breast roughly, and a scream tore from my throat, silenced by the gag. "I understand why he is wanting you. We will play with you later. If you stay alive."

Without another word, he scooped me up, and then I was being carried across to another car. There was a click, and I was dropped onto a hard surface, covered in a scratchy carpet material.

"Head down," the voice above instructed me.

The lid of the car boot was slammed shut, and I was surrounded by the stale scent of something distinctly metallic, combining with the petrol smell coming from the ropes that dug into my skin.

Trapped in the darkness, bound and gagged, useless tears fell, hot on my freezing skin.

"Be a good girl and scream for your boyfriend." The man holding me tore the gag from my mouth. Gasping, I sucked in a deep, fortifying breath. The rain combined with...sea air. We must be somewhere on the coast. I was disoriented, my head throbbing from the knocks I'd taken, but I wasn't about to go down without a fight. My arms were still bound, but I kicked out, throwing my head back at the same time. I connected with something hard, but there was no satisfying crack. All it served to do was for the man to grip me around the throat, snarling rage-filled words that I couldn't understand.

Everything became a blur as I struggled, white spots dancing in my vision as my lungs desperately worked to get air through the constricting hold on my throat. All I could hear was my pulse pounding in my ears, and I wasn't even aware of what was going on around me, my entire focus on escaping the man that held me down.

Then, suddenly, his weight was gone, and I was free. I crumpled to the ground, but reacting purely on instinct, I twisted my body to face the man. He was grappling with two men... I wiped my eyes. Was that Weston Cavendish? And Cassius Drummond? What were they doing here?

A glint of silver caught my eye, and I grabbed the screw-driver-type object from the ground. No one noticed me thrusting it up while Cassius held the man in a headlock and Weston punched him in the jaw. It pierced through denim and into flesh so easily, I dropped it in horror. A howl of rage came from the man, and he tore away from Cassius and Weston.

I shot upright with a gasp, my eyes flying open. My heart pounding, I blinked furiously until the room came into focus, before slumping back against the headboard.

I was in my bedroom. In my flat.

My eyes slowly scanned the room, taking in the features. It helped a little. Helped me to focus, to remember that while my flashback nightmares had really happened, it was over. Completely over. I started at the small Himalayan salt lamp next to my bed that I kept switched on because waking up from a nightmare only to find myself in the dark was something I didn't want to consider yet. Next, I scanned over my windows, covered with soft white curtains that dusted the floor. Then, across to the door that led to my walk-in wardrobe, over my dresser, past the door that led to my bathroom, and down to the soft, luxurious silvery carpet that covered the floor. Smoothing my hands over my white bedcovers, I breathed in and out deeply, until my heart rate slowed.

I allowed myself to remember what had happened after the point I'd been pulled from my nightmare, to remind myself that it was really all over.

Collapsing back onto the damp ground and closing my eyes, I let out a breath. Then another. Then another. A hand was placed on my back, and I flinched but settled when it remained there, a warm, steady pressure I could focus on.

"Jessa?"

His voice, normally so full of laughter and charm, was cracked and unsure. I tried to speak, but all I could manage was a whimpering sound.

"Jessa," he said again, and this time, his arms carefully came around me. Scooping me up, he lifted me to my feet. I clung to

him tightly, knowing that my legs would give way if I didn't have him to hold me up. "Fuck, you're freezing," he mumbled. He tried to move back, and I staggered. A huff escaped him, and then his arms tightened around me.

"Can you hold on for five seconds?" Carefully placing me down to lean against a metal surface, he directed my palms either side of me so I could brace myself against the side of the car. There was a rustling sound, and then I was surrounded by warmth as Cassius eased his hoodie over my head, draping it over my body.

"I'm taking her home," I heard Cassius say to someone, and then he was carrying me, not stopping until we reached his matte black SUV. He let go of me to open the door, and a panicked cry fell from my lips, completely involuntary.

"Jessa. I'm not going anywhere, okay? You're safe now. Safe with me."

His words were reassuring, and I managed a tiny nod before he helped me into the car and buckled up my seat belt.

I kept my hand resting lightly on the edge of his leg the whole journey back to my flat, needing to know he was still there. He seemed to understand, because he didn't comment. If I'd been in my right mind, none of this would have happened, yet now that I was away from danger, the fear that I'd been suppressing was drowning me in heavy, rolling waves, and only the feel of the warmth of his body under my hand was keeping the panic at bay.

When we reached my apartment building, he helped me inside, directing me to my sofa. After sitting me down, he pulled his phone from his pocket. It had been buzzing almost constantly while he'd been driving.

"Fuck. Cade—he's. Fuck. In hospital."

"You should go," I croaked out, closing my eyes so he couldn't see my terror at being left alone. It was clear I wasn't *successful in masking it when he dropped to his knees in front of me.*

"You really—"

I cut off whatever he was about to say. "It's fine, go. Caiden needs you. Weston needs your support."

The dilemma in his gaze was clear, but I knew that his loyalty was to his best friends, their bond stronger than anything I'd ever known. As it should be.

"Can... Do you want me to phone anyone to come over? Portia, maybe?"

I almost laughed at that. As if Portia would do anything that didn't benefit her in some way. "I'll be fine. Thank you." Injecting as much firmness as I could into my voice, I forced myself to meet his eyes.

There was no way he was convinced, but he sighed. "You've got my number. Text me anytime, okay?"

When I nodded, he rose to his feet with another sigh. He paused for a minute, then leaned down and kissed the top of my head. It was weirdly intimate, and I didn't know why. Maybe because my guard was down.

"Get some sleep. And text me," he commanded.

Then he was gone.

When the door closed behind him and I was left alone...that was when the tears began to fall.

With a sigh, I lay back down and closed my eyes. It had been months since the incident had happened, when Caiden had been shot, thankfully not fatally, and his step-mother had died. The Belarusian gang working with his stepmother was gone for good, and the docks where everything had taken place had been levelled, as if they were never there to begin with. I'd been dragged into the entire thing completely by mistake when Caiden's stepmother had been fed the wrong information, information that I was supposedly his girlfriend, even though we'd never been properly together like that.

Months since anything bad had happened. The nightmares were much less frequent now—and I'd finally been able to start sleeping again, with the help of my lamp and a white noise app on my phone.

But no matter how hard I tried to convince myself that everything was okay, no matter how much I reminded myself that I was fine, sleep didn't come for the rest of the night.

2

jessa

The next morning, I stumbled out of bed and into my bathroom. Looking at my reflection in the mirror after my shower, I sighed, thinking back to my life before the incident. You wouldn't know it to look at me now, with my tired eyes and dull, dark brown hair, but I used to be the girl everyone envied. Along with my former best friend, Portia, we'd ruled the halls of Alstone High, and then Alstone College, constantly surrounded by girls who wanted to be our friends because of our status. We hung out with the most popular boys, and life had been...easy, I suppose. My dad was of the sort to give me whatever I wanted without question as long as my grades remained high, so I'd enjoyed freedom and an almost unlimited supply of material things.

Then, everything had started to go wrong. It had begun with Winter Huntington showing up at Alstone College, turning Caiden Cavendish's head with her beauty. I'd hated her then, for stealing the attention of the most influential, hottest guys in Alstone. Caiden, his brother Weston,

Cassius Drummond, and their friend Zayde Lowry, collectively known as the Four.

To begin with, everything was normal, but it soon became clear that our position at the top was slipping. The Four picked Winter and became so protective of her, and they began to turn on me and Portia, bit by bit. We hadn't helped ourselves, if I was honest, and I really wasn't proud of my behaviour back then. At one point, Winter and I had almost ended up in a fight, but Caiden had come along and made it crystal clear to me and everyone else that he'd chosen her.

It hurt. Not so much because I wanted him, because although he was one of the hottest men I'd ever seen with his jet-black hair, gorgeous face, and sexy, tattooed body, there was never really any spark between us. It hurt because I'd wanted what he represented. Power. Status. Security. Social standing. All the things that had been important to me.

Everything had begun to fall apart. Portia was hiding something from me, and we were growing apart. When the incident had happened, I'd finally cracked and called her, after hours and hours of sitting there on my sofa, numb. Her only concern had been the fact that I was pulling out of our planned shopping trip to London. She never even gave me a chance to tell her what had happened. That had been the first nail in the coffin. The second nail was the first day she'd seen me after the incident, and she'd berated me for the way I looked.

"What happened to you? You look..."

The expression on her face was disgusted, her mouth opening and closing as she stood in my flat, clearly lost for words.

I took a deep breath. I needed to speak to someone about this. No one knew, except for those that had been there that night, and really only Cassius and Weston had actually seen me properly. Every time I thought about what had happened, my throat closed up, and my heart raced so fast that I grew light-headed.

"A man—"

"Was he hot?" Portia was suddenly in my face, her gaze fixed on me.

"No. No. Portia, he assaulted—"

"Don't want to hear it. If he wasn't hot, then forget him." She waved her hand in the air. "Are you actually going to put some makeup on?"

Suddenly angry, I glared at her. "No, I'm not."

Her eyes narrowed, and her lips thinned. "I see. You... Ever since your father started cosying up with the Cavendishes and Drummonds, you've been different. I suppose you think you're too good for me now, do you?

"What?" I stared at her. "No! I never said that."

She treated me to one of her disdainful looks. "You didn't have to say anything. It's obvious by this..." Her hand flicked up and down in my direction. "You can't even be bothered to make an effort."

"Portia, no. You're getting the wrong idea." My voice cracked, ice freezing my veins at the thought of my best friend abandoning me. And how fucking pathetic was that? I was Jessa De Witt, the girl that everyone wanted to be.

Hot tears filled my eyes.

"I've seen enough." Portia lifted her head, her mouth set in a flat line. "As far as I'm concerned, you can lose my number."

Then she turned on her heel and left, my apartment door slamming shut behind her.

The tears fell.

I'd never felt so alone.

. . .

Now Portia had moved away, for good, and I was left with the pieces of my life. I'd realised just how shallow my existence had been when my other so-called friends had drifted away in Portia's wake, and it was only my family name that had stopped me from becoming completely invisible.

The people I spoke to most these days, if you could call a group chat mostly consisting of memes "speaking," were Cassius, his sister, Lena, Winter's best friend, Kinslee, and Winter herself. Yes, Winter. We were far from friends, but after everything that had gone down, I guess you could say we were civil. Life was too short to hold a grudge.

I had a sneaking suspicion she pitied me, though, and that was a thought I couldn't stand. I made sure to avoid her in person, because being pitied—that would be the final nail in my coffin.

With all these thoughts whirling through my head, I pulled on a summer dress and flip-flops, taking my time to brush out my hair and apply a small amount of makeup for the first time in a long time. The sun was shining outside, and as I stepped out of the front door, pulling on my sunglasses, I could almost convince myself that I was okay.

Almost.

Firmly pushing everything from my mind, I made a beeline for the apartment block car park where my grey Mercedes S560 was parked. Once inside, I hit my half-brother's name in my contacts list and sent him a quick message.

Me: On my way. Don't forget our lunch date

He replied immediately, which was surprising in a way.

Austin De Witt was always busy running his empire. He'd decided not to go into the family business, instead building up his own company that he'd started from scratch, first in the drinks industry, making a name for himself with a small range of spirits, and now he'd expanded by way of a merger with another company to run his own nightclub with an attached bar, right in the middle of prime London territory. All that, and he'd only just turned twenty-four. I had big shoes to fill.

Austin: Haven't forgotten. See you soon

Dropping my phone to the passenger seat, I let a small smile cross my face.

After checking myself in the car mirror to make sure I looked presentable, because Austin would ask too many questions if I showed up without perfect hair and makeup, I started up the engine. I headed into central London and down to the sushi restaurant close to my brother's bar. I'd suggested meeting at his bar, but he wanted to be away from his workplace.

"I ordered for you," was his greeting when the hostess showed me to our table, tucked away in a corner of the restaurant. He flashed me a quick grin, all white teeth and tanned skin, and I smiled, relaxing. Even though my brother could be a bit standoffish at times, and we didn't see each other often, he still looked out for me, and I knew he cared.

As we ate, we made small talk about my degree course, and he told me about a new gin he was acquiring for his brand. I found myself relaxing, my troubles melting away as we talked.

"The final part of the merger's going ahead," he told me

when we were finishing up the last of our food. "I'll soon be working out of that building there." Lifting his finger, he indicated towards a huge, shiny skyscraper. "The whole place is new."

"I hope you asked for a corner office," I said absent-mindedly. Something out of the corner of my eye had caught my attention. The back of a head—pale, shaved hair—something about it tugged at my gut. I shifted in my seat uneasily.

"I couldn't talk Creed into a corner office, but my view is insane," my brother was saying, but I barely heard him. My ears were ringing, my whole body frozen, as the man who'd caught my eye turned around and I saw the scar running down one cheek, those flinty eyes, and that harsh face that starred in my nightmares.

It was *him*.

The man who'd taken me captive.

The man I'd thought was dead.

Petr Ivanov.

Somehow, I managed to hold on to my composure while Austin paid the bill and we said our goodbyes. Lucky for me, he was distracted by a business call, and after a quick kiss to my cheek and a muttered promise to talk to me later, he disappeared. My heart racing, I melted into the lunchtime crowds, scanning everywhere for a glimpse of a shaved head. When I reached my car, I slid inside, thankful for the automatic locking, and with shaking hands, pulled out my phone.

I navigated straight to Cassius' number. Tears blurred my vision as I typed out the simple text.

Me: Petr's here

My phone rang almost instantly, Cassius' name flashing across the screen. I hit the speaker button and sat back, closing my eyes.

"Jessa? What was that text supposed to mean?"

"I just saw him. You-you told me he was *dead*." My words were accusing, but my voice broke, and I bit the inside of my cheek, unwilling to allow myself to cry in front of him.

"Where are you?" His voice gave nothing away. "Where did you see him?"

"You told me he was dead," I repeated, my throat swollen with the tears I was holding back.

"Can you meet?"

"Y-yes."

I heard him sigh softly. "Come to my house."

The drive back to Alstone was made on autopilot. My head was spinning. Had I actually seen him, or was it a figment of my imagination? Cassius had told me he was dead, after all. I needed answers, and now. I was only just beginning to drag myself out of the nightmares, and there was no way I was going back.

Pulling up outside the huge house that the Four shared, I sat for a minute, gathering myself.

Then, I climbed out of my car, stepped up to the door, and knocked.

3

cassius

"It's for me," I shouted, diving for the front door before anyone else could get there. When I flung the door open, Jessa was standing with her hand still raised.

She looked...different to the way she'd been lately. She looked like the old Jessa. Polished and sexy as fuck. But when I looked into her deep green eyes, there was a haunted expression that had never been there before she'd been taken.

Snapping back into my default mode, I gave her a wide grin, bowing. "Welcome to my humble abode."

She didn't even comment, which told me how serious she was. I let the grin fall from my face as I led her through the house and into the lounge. All my other housemates were in the garden, which was good, since there was a high chance that she'd shout at me, and I didn't need an audience for that.

As soon as she'd taken a seat on one of the sofas, I threw myself down across from her and picked up the thread of our phone conversation. "Where did you see him? Are you sure it was him?"

Her eyes narrowed, darkening and flashing with anger. Was it weird that I welcomed it, because it chased away that haunted look? "So he *is* alive. Why did you tell me he was dead?"

"Uh." I rubbed the back of my head. "Technically, I didn't. I told you he was gone. That they were all gone."

"That implies that they were dead! You know, like everyone else involved was! What else was a lie?" Her voice was raised in anger, and I shot a quick glance at the lounge door, crossing my fingers that West wouldn't choose this moment to show up.

"Nothing was a lie. The others *are* dead. Littlefinger—I mean, Petr...he was badly injured, and he fled the country, or so I heard." I leaned forwards, my voice softening. "I didn't want you to worry. I didn't think there was any chance of him coming back."

Her shoulders slumped, and her composure slipped. "I thought...I wish... If he's alive, that means I didn't imagine it. He was really there."

I climbed off my chair and went to sit next to her, placing a careful hand on her shoulder. If this had been anyone else, I wouldn't have hesitated to hug them or whatever, but this was Jessa. Even though we'd been communicating on and off in our group chat, even I knew that memes weren't enough to build a bridge between us. Deep down, I was still pissed off with her for the way she'd treated Winter, even if it seemed like Winter had forgiven her. But I pushed that thought aside for now.

"Tell me what happened," I commanded softly.

Staring down at her hands that were clasped in her lap, she related how she'd seen him outside the restaurant, just a brief glimpse, but it was enough to convince her. I had my doubts about whether she'd really seen him or just thought she had, but if there was a chance he was back in the country, then it needed to be investigated. There would be no reason why he'd come back to Alstone—there was nothing here for him now, but even so, he was a sneaky fucker, and someone needed to keep an eye on him.

"I'll make some enquiries," I promised. "Give me the location where you saw him, and I'll see what I can find out."

"Okay." She nodded, scrolling to the maps app on her phone and screenshotting the restaurant details for me. "Thanks," she added, almost as an afterthought. She stood, letting my hand slip off her shoulder, and met my eyes quickly before looking away.

"I'd better go."

I'd seen the fear in her gaze, that same fear I'd seen when I left her back in her apartment, all those months ago. She was scared to be alone, no doubt shaken by what had happened today.

I'd had to leave her alone that time, because Caiden was unconscious in hospital, bleeding from a bullet wound, but this time, I didn't have to.

Standing, I gripped her arm lightly. "Stay."

Her eyes flew back to mine, and she stared at me silently for a long moment. Then she gave a tiny nod.

"Okay."

She stepped behind me as we walked through the open doors that led out onto the deck, almost like she was hiding. Which was understandable, I guess, since none of us were actually friends with her, and she wasn't exactly likely to receive a warm welcome.

Everyone was lazing around down on the grass, recovering from the water fight we'd just had. As well as my best friends and housemates, Weston, Caiden, and Zayde, we lived with Caiden's girlfriend, Winter, and as of a few days ago, my sister, Lena, who was the girlfriend of my best friend, Weston.

When I stepped down from the deck with Jessa in tow, everyone fell silent.

"Jessa's here," I announced unnecessarily.

I heard Cade mutter, "You don't say," while rolling his eyes, clearly displeased, so I decided that I might as well make the big announcement, if only to stop everyone staring at Jessa, who was looking at the grass like it was the most interesting thing she'd ever seen.

"Littlefinger's back." I widened my eyes dramatically. "Might be back," I added when everyone just stared at me with their mouths open.

"Why do you call him that?" Jessa's voice was quiet, almost in my ear.

"Long story. Mostly because the tip of his finger's missing."

"Makes sense."

I flashed her a quick grin, which she automatically returned before seemingly remembering where she was. She dropped her gaze back to the ground, and I gave a loud sigh. Why was no one saying anything?

"Didn't you hear me?" I tried again, this time enunciating every word slowly. "Little. Finger. Is. Back."

Eventually, Winter broke the silence, her brow furrowed. "Back? As in, here? And why do I get the feeling this has something to do with Jessa?" Pushing her sunglasses to the top of her head, she eyed Jessa unhappily, not that I could blame her. I wasn't exactly happy about this whole situation, either.

Since it didn't look like Jessa was about to talk, I gave them a quick rundown, and even as I was speaking, Z was climbing to his feet. He muttered something about speaking to Creed about it, and I nodded, sparing him a brief glance as he headed in the direction of the house.

West straightened up, carefully dislodging my sister's head from his thigh. As she sat up, he stood, crossing over to me. "Want me to make some enquiries?"

From behind him, Lena cleared her throat pointedly. "If you're hacking into anything, you'd better not leave me out."

"As if I would," he shot back, holding out his hand to her with a smile. I'd just about got used to seeing them together. Yeah, it still seemed a bit weird sometimes—but they were both so fucking happy, it was clear to anyone that they belonged together. Even if they were my best friend and my sister.

When they headed inside and it was just Caiden and Winter left, I lowered myself to the ground, pulling a still silent Jessa down with me. She stumbled, bracing herself on my arm, her fingers curling around my bicep as she steadied herself.

"Watch it," she hissed, shooting me a glare, which made me grin.

When I turned back to Cade and Winter, they were both glancing at each other. Caiden had sunglasses on, so I couldn't make out his expression, but his jaw was set in his moody-bugger mode, which meant I'd probably need to do damage control. Steeling myself, I waited for it, Jessa completely still next to me, and I could feel the tension in her body where her bare arm was brushing against mine.

Caiden turned his focus towards Jessa, and I instinctively moved my hand to lay my fingers over hers, which were gripping a handful of the grass.

"I don't want you here."

Winter elbowed him, hard, and he grunted, shooting her a quick look before continuing. "I don't want you here, but I'm—" His face twisted before he finally managed to get the words out. "—willing to put the past shit behind us. You upset my girlfriend in any way, and you're out. No second chances."

"Fucking hell, you hold a grudge." I rubbed my thumb over Jessa's fingers, a quick, reassuring gesture that I didn't even think about before removing my hand and leaning back on my arms.

"Can you blame me?" Now he'd said his piece to Jessa, he carried on like she wasn't even there. "She constantly tried it on with me even when I'd made it crystal fucking clear that I was into Winter. And she was a bitch to Winter, you can't even deny it."

"Wait a minute. What about the whole kissing at the party shit?"

In unison, Winter and Jessa both winced, and Caiden's mouth fell open.

Fuck.

I should *not* have brought that up.

Caiden ripped his sunglasses off, glaring at me. "What, where you had your hands all over my girlfriend and kissed her for five minutes straight?"

"It was hardly five minutes, mate. More like five seconds. She wasn't even your girlfriend at the time—you were still pretending you didn't want her, remember?" I raised a brow at him, and he bared his teeth. "Cade." I lowered my voice, eyeing him cautiously. "I thought we were past this. I didn't think you still held a grudge against me."

Abruptly, his anger vanished almost as fast as it had come. He rubbed his hand across his face with a groan. "I don't." His eyes met mine. "I *don't*. Fuck, mate. That was unfair of me."

"You used me." Jessa spoke quietly, her focus on Caiden. "You made me think that I had a chance with you." There was no accusation in her voice, just resignation. "I know I made things worse."

"I used you." Winter spoke up as her eyes met mine, and I shrugged. It was true, in a way, but it had been my idea to begin with.

"This better not turn into a fucking therapy session," Caiden warned, but I was barely paying attention, my mind going back to the party.

I tugged Winter down onto the sofa next to me, keeping my eye on Cade, who was taunting Winter with his bare torso on display, acting like she wasn't even in the room. Winter's eyes tracked every movement he made, and her entire body stiffened as Jessa threw her arms around him. When he hugged her back, giving Winter an acidic look, I sighed.

"Oh, it's like that, is it?" Picking up the blunt that was lying on the coffee table ready for me, I leaned into Winter. "Watch what he does, and be ready to act." After lighting the blunt, I passed it to her, keeping an eye on Cade and Jessa.

"Who is that?" Winter didn't even have a hope of disguising the jealousy in her voice. Her hand shook almost imperceptibly as she lifted the blunt to her lips.

I looked between her and Jessa. Seemed that Cade had a type. Both of them were fucking beautiful, with gorgeous bodies and long dark hair, although Jessa's fell straight down her back while Winter's was currently in loose waves.

"Jessa," I replied to her question. "She's alright. Maybe not

to you," I added as Jessa spun to face us with a bitchy little smile directed at Winter while Cade continued to paw at her.

A flash of Jessa on her knees, sucking my dick with her talented mouth, burned through me, and I added, almost unthinkingly, "She sucks cock like a fucking porn star." As soon as I'd said the words, I instantly regretted them, but there was no taking them back now. We both watched as Cade and Jessa started kissing, and a wave of anger hit me, completely unexpected. What the fuck was Cade playing at? Winter didn't deserve this shit. He'd be lucky to have her. She shouldn't even be giving him the time of day based on the way he'd acted towards her, but unfortunately for me, she was actually into him and he was into her, although they both had the worst case of denial I'd ever seen. Unfortunate for me, because if Cade wasn't one of my best mates, I'd make a move on Winter. She was the first girl I'd ever had more than a passing interest in, and because of Cade, she was completely off-limits.

Winter was similarly affected, because she suddenly downed the beer she was holding and slammed the bottle down on the table. "Fuck him."

I glanced at her approvingly. "That's the spirit, babe. Let's give him a taste of his own medicine, yeah?"

She didn't even hesitate in her reply. "Yes."

Okay. I was going to do the charitable thing and sacrifice myself for the greater good. After a final drag of the blunt, I dropped it in the ashtray and gently tugged Winter onto me, placing my arms around her waist. Fuck. My primary objective was blurring, and my focus was narrowing to the feel of her in my arms, her chest rising and falling with shallow breaths as she stared at Caiden with Jessa. Dipping my head to her ear, I murmured, "Tell me if you want me to stop, at any point, okay?"

She nodded, her eyes falling closed, and I chanced a quick look at Cade to remind myself why I was doing this. His gaze *bounced between the two of us, his eyes darkening, and I smiled. Time to see how far I could push him before he snapped. Lowering my head, I pressed kisses to Winter's neck and down to her shoulder.*

"Sometimes I wish you weren't Caiden's."

"I'm not Caiden's," she replied automatically.

Even if neither of them wanted to admit it, and even if at that moment I wished she was mine, she was his. "You are. But since he's in denial and playing dirty, I get to play with you." I stroked over the soft, smooth skin of her thighs. Bad idea. My dick, already way too fucking interested by the hot girl in my lap, perked up even further, and I had to fall back on my patented boner-killer scenario of my old schoolteacher naked. Leaning forwards, I swiped my beer bottle from the table and downed it while I wrestled myself back under control.

A soft gasp fell from Winter's lips, and there was so much hurt in it that I couldn't stand it. My gaze shot to Caiden, his hands all over Jessa's lush tits as he stared at us with rage written all over his face. This was beyond fucked up.

Spinning Winter around so she was facing me and strad-dling my thighs, I gave in to the rising desire and slanted my lips over hers. She opened her mouth to me instantly, throwing herself into the kiss like she was trying to convince herself that it meant something, but I knew that she didn't think of me as anything more than a friend.

Without warning, she was suddenly ripped away from me, and Caiden was dragging her out of the room.

Job done.

But I felt so fucking empty.

I slumped back on the sofa, closing my eyes. The cushion dipped next to me, but I remained as I was.

"Looks like we both got rejected." The soft voice next to me was laced with bitterness. "What does she have that I don't?"

Jessa sounded genuinely baffled, and I peeled my eyes open, turning my head towards her. I concentrated on the first part of her question.

"Babe. We don't get rejected. Look at us. It's just not possible."

A tiny smile crossed her face. "Your ego knows no bounds." But the smile remained when I lit up another blunt, handing it to her, so I chalked it up as a win.

We finished up the blunt, and she even helped herself to one of my beers. I had a good buzz going on when she turned her head to face me. My gaze dropped to her lips, and I found myself leaning forwards, closing the distance between us. She sighed, her breath ghosting across my mouth, her hand sliding onto my thigh.

The next second, she stiffened, her eyes darting behind me, and she leapt away. "I'm going to go home." I didn't even have a chance to reply before she was gone. Turning my head in the direction she'd been looking, I saw Caiden, minus Winter. He wasn't even looking at me, but yeah...Jessa had probably had the right idea. Not sure if I wanted to push Cade that much. I'd already kissed one of the girls he'd been with tonight. Jessa wasn't the only unattached girl here, not by a long shot.

With my mind made up, I climbed to my feet and headed in the direction of the kitchen. Time to get another drink and see what, or who, my options were.

4

jessa

I could tell Cassius was lost in thought by the way his eyes went all unfocused. I'd tried to put that night out of my mind, as I had with everything that involved Caiden and Winter... In fact, I'd tried to put *everything* out of my mind.

Turning to Caiden, I replied to his earlier statement about not wanting me around and not upsetting Winter. I knew his comments were fair. The old me would've made a cutting remark, uncaring of what he thought, but that night at the docks had changed me in ways I was only beginning to realise. "I know you don't want me here, and that's fair." Swallowing hard, I forced myself to continue. "I don't have any intention of hurting Winter, okay?" I flashed her a small smile before I decided to push Caiden, just a tiny bit. "I know you think you're irresistible to all women, but that ship has sailed. You know that it was mostly our families pushing us together, right?"

He narrowed his eyes at me, his mouth flattening into a thin line, but all he did was respond with a sharp nod. Winter squeezed his leg gently before meeting my gaze.

"Well, I for one don't hold a grudge. I'm not sure if we'll ever be friends, but for what it's worth, I'm sorry about everything that happened." She gave me a genuine smile. Argh. Why did she have to be so *nice*? It made me feel even worse about the way I'd treated her.

"Thanks," I murmured, not sure how else to respond.

Caiden got to his feet, pulling Winter up with him. "I need a beer." They disappeared in the direction of the house, and I let out a shaky breath. I'd never felt intimidated by him before, by any of them, but I guess I *was* here at their home, and we didn't have the buffer of being surrounded by other people like the other times I'd interacted with them. Caiden was throwing off some seriously hostile vibes, and none of them seemed happy that I was there. Again, understandable. Even Cassius...he hadn't been hostile, but his usual flirty banter wasn't there.

"Why did you invite me to hang out with you? Why are you being nice to me but acting weird? Why did you set up that group chat with me?" The questions suddenly came pouring out of me in a rush.

He let himself fall backwards onto the grass, flinging a hand over his eyes to shade them from the sun. "I don't know?"

"Cass."

A hugely exaggerated sigh came from him, making his chest rise and his muscles come into sharp definition under his T-shirt. Fuck, Cassius Drummond was completely mouth-watering. All dirty-blond hair, bright blue eyes that were always full of humour, an easy grin, and all those gorgeous defined muscles wrapped in skin golden from the sun, his arms decorated with swirling tattoos. And his cock...

I gasped, sitting bolt upright. After the incident at the

docks, I'd lost all interest in...well, most things, actually, but sex especially. And now, here I was, admiring Cassius in a very non-platonic way, and thinking of his dick...

My heart beat faster, hope and excitement building inside me. If I could feel like this, maybe it meant I was finally beginning to move on. To be *me* again. Or whatever this new version of me was.

"Jessa?"

My gaze flew to his to see him staring at me curiously, and I felt my cheeks heat. There was no way I was about to explain what had just happened. "Please, explain," I said, trying to get the conversation back on track.

He groaned. "I felt bad about what happened to you, okay? I saw what you were like that day I left you. That's why I set up the chat, and that's why I invited you to stay today."

"What about the acting weird thing?"

"I'm not acting weird."

"You are." When he shook his head, confused, I tried to explain. "You're not treating me like you used to. I don't know, it's just—wait, you feel bad about what happened? So you feel sorry for me or something, is that it?"

Huffing out a frustrated breath, he ran his hand down his face. "Y-no. I don't bloody know."

"Look, I don't need sympathy. Please don't treat me any differently. I want to get back to normal, and I want..." My words trailed off. What did I want from him? Nothing, really. He didn't owe me anything. "Never mind. Just don't go around feeling sorry for me."

Rolling onto his side, he stared at me for a minute, tugging his bottom lip between his teeth. "Normal. Right," he said eventually. There was another long silence, and then he reached out and ran two of his fingers through the lengths of my hair that were falling down the length of my upper arm. "Is this you getting back to normal?" He tugged lightly on my hair, then released it. A weird little shiver went through me, but I brushed it off.

"This was me meeting my brother for lunch and not wanting an interrogation about my appearance, so I made an effort," I told him honestly. "He's used to me looking a certain way, and I really didn't feel like telling him about everything that had happened, especially now it's all over."

Or I'd thought it had been over. Dread crept through me again as I was reminded that the source of my nightmares was back in England.

"You're looking very good, Jessa." Cassius' voice lowered, taking on a husky tone, and my eyes widened, all thoughts of Petr Ivanov disappearing in an instant. His fingers trailed down my arm, setting off a chain of goose-bumps wherever he touched. "Your dress looks a bit uncomfortable. Why don't you let me help you take it off?"

It took me a couple of seconds to realise what he'd said, and then I shoved at him, sending him onto his back. "You're a dickhead sometimes." An unwilling smile appeared on my face.

"You wanted normal, babe. Don't blame me for giving you what you asked for." He spoke through his laughter, and I shoved at him again, partly irritated but mostly relieved. I didn't want to be treated like I was fragile.

Gripping my arms, he yanked me into him. "You're gonna pay for pushing me. Twice." Then he dug his fingers into my sides and began tickling me.

A scream tore from my throat. "Stop! Please! You're torturing me!" I managed to get out, laughing breathlessly, trying to scramble away from his fingers. Instead of releasing me, he spun us so that I was lying on my back in the grass, and he had me pinned under him, still tickling me mercilessly through fits of laughter. "I'll do anything!" I cried, not even able to attempt to throw him off me. The tickling had made me too weak. It was pure torture.

"Anything?" Finally stilling his fingers but keeping his grip on me, he raised his head to meet my gaze, his blue eyes sparkling with humour.

"Anything. Just stop this torture."

His thumbs stroked over my sides, and then he dipped down, placing a lightning-quick, completely unexpected kiss to my lips. I froze for a second, but then with a shake of his head and his trademark grin, the moment passed. "How's that for normal?" He climbed off me, taking a seat on the grass next to me again.

Taking a moment to catch my breath and compose myself, I cleared my throat, staring at the tree line in front of me that marked the boundary of the Four's outside space. "I could do without the tickling. But...thanks, I suppose."

"I aim to please."

His smile died away at the approach of Zayde. Zayde didn't look at me, focusing his attention on Cassius.

"He's back."

At Zayde's words, my stomach churned, and I dragged my knees up, curling my body over them and resting my head on my arms. This was ridiculous. Why was I acting this way, when the likelihood of me actually running into Petr was miniscule? I could stay away from London. Maybe Austin would have something to say if I cancelled what we'd agreed would become semi-regular lunch dates, but he could always come to Alstone for a change if he could drag himself away from the city.

"Creed couldn't get involved before since the Strelichevos had ties to the Volkovs, but now it seems like he might've gone rogue."

Nothing Zayde was saying made any sense to me, except for the final part of his sentence.

It seems like he might've gone rogue.

All my senses were on high alert. Those premonitions that you sometimes get, that you really shouldn't ignore? That's what I was having, right then. A very strong premonition, a sense that I was in danger, even though it made no sense. Why would I be targeted, anyway? The docks incident had been a case of mistaken identity, and I'd just been in the wrong place at the wrong time.

A tiny whimper escaped me before I clamped my lips shut, but it was too late. Both Cassius' and Zayde's heads turned in my direction.

Cassius pursed his lips, looking back at Zayde. "We'll talk about this more later." Then he turned back to me. "Do you want to go home?"

I nodded, even though everything inside of me was screaming that I didn't want to be left alone. But these people weren't really my friends. They didn't owe me anything. Cassius had gone above and beyond already, all things considered.

"Try not to worry," he said as I opened my car door with a shaking hand. "We'll find out what we can, but there's no reason why he would come here. You're safe. He has no reason to come after you."

Those were almost the same words that I'd told myself earlier, but hearing them from Cassius didn't make them any more believable.

When I was back in my flat, I locked the door and pulled the deadbolt across, closing all the curtains and blinds and flipping all the lights on. Turning the TV up to a slightly higher volume than normal, I collapsed onto my sofa with a glass of water, trying to lose myself in reality TV.

When a loud knock came at the door, I startled, knocking my glass of water over, the contents spreading across the floor. My heart pounding, I stayed completely still until the knock sounded again.

I forced my suddenly shaking legs to cooperate, creeping over to the door and looking through the peephole. Relief left me breathless as I saw the familiar figure of James Granville standing in the corridor. He lived in my apartment building and was also one of my fellow students.

Undoing the deadbolt and the lock, I opened the door a crack and attempted a smile. "James. How can I help you?"

He scrutinised me closely, concern in his gaze. "Are you okay?"

"Fine."

There was silence for a moment, but then he eventually shrugged. "Okay." He lifted his hand, passing me a small brown envelope. "Here. This has your name on it, but it got put into my mailbox by mistake."

"Thanks." I took it from him, and he gave me a brief smile.

"Anytime. I, uh..." He pointed back down the hallway in the direction of the stairs.

"Yeah. See you later, James." Closing the door softly, I locked and bolted it again, then padded across to my sofa. I'd forgotten about the spilled water, and I groaned as the liquid soaked through my fluffy socks. Pulling them off, I curled up with my feet out of the danger zone, then turned my attention to the envelope. The front had *Miss Dewitt* written in a messy black biro scrawl, and I frowned as I turned it over, sliding my thumb into the gap to ease it open.

There was only one thing in the envelope.

A photo.

My eyes traced over the image. The coil of rope and a piece of rough brown material. And at the bottom? An all too familiar screwdriver-type object, the very tip of it dipping into a deep liquid stain the colour of blood.

It was a message.

Very, very slowly, I laid the photo down on the arm of the sofa and, just as slowly, picked up my phone. It took me three tries to unlock it, and then I navigated to the camera. Snapping a photo, I sent it to Cassius along with four words that as I wrote them sent icy shivers of fear through my bloodstream.

He's here for me.

5

cassius

When my phone buzzed with a message, I was in the student union bar with a gorgeous redhead in my lap and her blonde friend perched on the arm of the chair next to us. Things were looking up. There had been no new information on Littlefinger, and other than Z's cryptic comment about him going rogue, no one seemed to think he was a serious threat. I didn't, either. So what if he was in London? There was no way he'd show his face in Alstone. Everyone that he'd been connected to here was either dead or gone, and unless he was completely fucking insane, he wouldn't even try coming near us.

I downed the rest of my drink, shifting the girl on my lap so I could dig my phone out of my pocket. Handing her my empty glass, I skimmed my fingers up her thigh while I unlocked my phone with my other hand.

The message alert showed Jessa's name, and I groaned internally. What now? I almost didn't read it, but I knew that I probably should, just in case. There was a photo of what looked like a load of junk and a message that just said *He's here for me*.

Frowning, I enlarged the photo. What the fuck? Where had this come from?

I sat still for a moment, thinking, before I sighed. Leaning forwards, I spoke in the redhead's ear, making sure that my tone conveyed just how regretful I was. "K—" Shit, I'd forgotten her name. "Babe, I'm gonna have to take a rain check. Something's come up."

She turned her head, pouting, and I stuck my bottom lip out, widening my eyes. The look never failed to get me sympathy, and it was no different this time, either. Her pout disappeared, and she gave me a sympathetic smile. "It's okay. These things happen. I'll give you my number. Text me when you're free."

While she input her number into my phone and then passed my phone to her friend to do the same, I glanced around the bar, seeing if I could spot West. He'd arrived with me, but he'd disappeared off to somewhere with his friend Rumi, avoiding the single girls who'd always flocked around us both before he got together with my sister. The bonus of this situation was that there were more girls for me to choose from now he was no longer available, although right now the bar was fairly quiet since the semester was over and a lot of the students had gone home for the summer.

It didn't take me long to spot him, playing pool with Rumi, and I huffed out a relieved breath. Once I'd retrieved my phone from the girls, I shifted the redhead from my thighs and stood. I did the gentlemanly thing and gave both her and her friend a kiss before I left, leaving them smiling after me as I walked away with a final wink at them.

"Look." Stopping by the pool table, I spoke to my best mate in a low voice, shielding my phone from anyone else's view.

He stared at the screen, then at me, unimpressed. "What. You want a round of applause for getting yet another girl's number?"

"Huh?" My gaze flew down, where my phone was showing my newest contacts. "No, shit...hang on..." When I navigated to the message, I enlarged the photo and shoved my phone in his face. He studied it intently, his brows pulled together.

"This is to do with Littlefinger?"

"I think so, yeah, but I don't know what it means. I'm gonna step outside and try and get hold of Jessa, find out what's going on."

"Keep me updated."

With an affirmative nod, I left him there, heading outside. Hitting Jessa's number, I lifted my phone to my ear.

"Sorry. I panicked." Her voice was breathless with the undercurrent of fear that gave me an unwanted flashback to the night at the docks.

"Do you wanna explain what this picture's all about? Where did it come from?"

"I-it was in my mailbox. Or it was supposed to be anyway. It got put in James Granville's by mistake, but it was in an envelope addressed to me. I think it's from *him*."

"Wait a second. He knows where you live?"

I heard her shaky intake of breath before she replied. "Yeah. He took me from my apartment building that night."

That was all I needed to hear. For some reason, I'd never thought about the fact that Littlefinger would know where Jessa lived. But yeah, he knew, and he'd sent her a message. I had a sick feeling that it was supposed to unnerve her, to tell her that he knew exactly where she was and that she wasn't safe. It meant that either he was back in Alstone or someone else was helping him out. Either way, I wasn't happy with the thought of Jessa staying in that apartment building.

It wasn't my responsibility to take charge here, but at the same time, I was culpable in a way. If it hadn't been for our investigations, none of this would have happened to her—and my best friends and I were the ones there that night. I wasn't happy with sending Jessa to her dad's house, either—from what I knew of him, he lived alone and wasn't at home much, and the thought of her being all on her own in that huge house didn't sit right with me. Who was to say she'd be any safer there?

"Pack a bag. You're coming to stay with me until we get this shit sorted out. Be there soon," I told her, ending the call before she could disagree with me. Swiping across the screen, I ordered an Uber, then tapped out a quick text to West to let him know I was leaving.

Twenty minutes later, I was inside Jessa's flat, eyeing her as she stood on her rug, hugging her arms to herself and staring at me with wide, fearful eyes. She'd changed since she'd left my place earlier, and she was barefoot, in simple navy Nike jogging bottoms and a sleeveless black top, her face free of makeup.

Her eyes lowered, and her voice was small. "Do you really want me to stay with you?"

That was a question with a complicated answer, so I countered it with a question of my own. "Do you want to stay here?"

She immediately shook her head, chewing her lip. Her gaze had that haunted look again, and I hated it.

"Good. Bag packed?"

"Almost."

"We can come back for anything you forget. Or I can, if you like." With a shrug, I picked up the suitcase standing by the front door. Jessa took one last glance around, then picked up her handbag from the coffee table and hefted her laptop bag over her other shoulder. After sliding her shoes on and flicking off the lights, she followed me out of the door.

When we arrived back at my house after a silent journey, she finally spoke as we unloaded her stuff from her Mercedes.

"I hope I wasn't dragging you away from anything important tonight."

I shot her a smirk, closing her car boot and picking up her case. "Nah. I could've had a girl...two girls, in fact, but I got their numbers, so it's all good. I can pick up where we left off later."

"Sorry."

"Don't worry, my little cockblocker. I sacrificed my pleasure for the greater good."

An amused, or possibly disgusted, noise came from her throat, and that haunted look lessened. "I was feeling bad about it until you just said that."

Laughing with a weird sense of relief, I opened the front door and directed her inside. "If you're feeling bad, you can always take their place."

"I'm not feeling that bad, but I'll keep it in mind," she said dryly as she followed me up the stairs. We ended up on the upstairs landing, and I pointed out the bedrooms. I was pretty sure she knew where mine and Caiden's were, at the very least, but it had been a long time since she'd been in this part of the house.

I hadn't been home since I'd made my suggestion that

she could stay, so I was prepared for the guest room to be a mess. But when I opened the door, it was actually clear, even though it had been a bit of a junk room before. Come to think of it, Winter had mentioned something about clearing out the spare rooms when Lena was due to move in, so I guess I had her to thank.

"You can sleep here. There's a lock on the door, and you get a bathroom. Towels are in there." That was a guess, but if the room was ready to sleep in, I was assuming the bathroom would be stocked.

"Okay. Thanks." She dropped her bags to the floor and walked over to the bed, taking a seat on the edge. Her eyes met mine, her gaze cautious. "Do the others know I'm staying?"

"Not yet, but I'll tell them." They'd probably have something to say about it, but my plan was to hide Jessa up in the guest room and get everyone to do shots, then spring the news on them when they were drunk.

One raised brow was the only reaction I got. "I'll try and get some rest," she said softly, and I took the hint.

"See you tomorrow." I left her to it and headed downstairs to see who was around. West was still out, and so was Lena, but Cade and Z were in the lounge on our new PS5, while Winter was curled up reading.

"Shots, anyone?"

Winter glanced up from her Kindle and pointed towards the full mugs on the coffee table. "I just made drinks. Do you want me to make you one?"

"No, thanks. I'll get my own." Guess that plan wasn't going to work. Maybe it was better to just come out and tell them. Wandering into the kitchen, I grabbed a glass from the cupboard and filled it with water from the tap, staring unseeingly at the window.

"Hi."

A reflection appeared in the window next to me, and I jumped a fucking mile, accompanied by the sound of breaking glass as it slipped out of my hand and dropped into the sink.

"Fuck!"

"Sorry, I didn't mean to make you jump. I just came down for a glass of water." Jessa was staring at me, and even though I was only looking at her reflection, I could see she was struggling not to laugh, biting down on her lip.

Glaring at her reflection, I reached into the sink with both hands to scoop up the broken glass.

I should've fucking looked.

Both of my thumbs somehow managed to jab into the jagged broken edges.

"Fuck! Fuckfuckfuck!"

At my shout of pain, there was a stampede as Caiden, Zayde, and Winter all came bursting into the room. Nice to know they cared, I guess.

"What's Jessa doing here?"

I panicked at Cade's dangerously low tone and spun around to face them, brandishing my injured hands. "My thumbs! Look at my thumbs!"

Everyone's focus swung to me, and then they all started speaking at once, apart from Jessa, who looked like she was losing the battle to hide her laughter.

"Stop dripping blood all over the floor. It's unhygienic."

"It's only a scratch."

"Are you okay?"

Shooting an amused Jessa a death glare, I turned my attention to Winter, who was the only one showing any kind of sympathy. "It hurts."

She shook her head. "You're so dramatic sometimes."

Maybe not as sympathetic as I'd originally thought. I wasn't even lying—the cuts fucking stung.

She stepped a bit closer, her genuine concern for me overriding everything else. Lifting my hands, she examined my thumbs, biting her lip before a thoughtful expression came over her face. "The cuts aren't deep, but we should get them cleaned up. Jessa?" She turned to Jessa. All traces of amusement were instantly wiped from her face, and she eyed Winter with caution. Winter glanced over at me, then back to Jessa. "In the upstairs main bathroom, there's a first aid kit on the top shelf of the tall white cabinet. Please could you get it?"

Jessa nodded once, practically flying out of the room. As soon as she was gone, Caiden spoke up again. "Explain."

Winter directed my hands under the tap, cleaning the cuts with lukewarm water. I thought about ignoring my nosy friends, but I couldn't avoid them for much longer. "Jessa's staying over," I said finally, aware of three sets of eyes on me. "More Littlefinger shit. It seems like we have more to worry about than we thought." I gave them a rundown of the situation, and by the end of it, everyone looked even more unhappy.

"I don't like anything about this." Caiden paced up and down, doing his best impression of a thundercloud. He did a dramatic spin on his heel, whirling round to me, and I barely contained my eye roll at his theatrics. "I don't like *her* being here."

"You think any of us do?" I snapped, losing my patience.

Winter cleared her throat loudly, widening her eyes at me, and I winced, turning my head to see Jessa standing in the doorway, clasping the first aid kit with a stricken look on her face.

Shit.

She took a visibly deep breath, straightening her shoulders, then headed into the now completely silent kitchen and handed Winter the first aid kit. Her green eyes met mine, so wide and so fucking sad that something inside me twisted painfully. "I know none of you want me here. I...I'll make sure I stay out of everyone's way. You won't even know I'm here." Her voice wobbled as her whispered words fell from her in a rush.

She was gone before I could explain that I'd been replying to the first part of Caiden's comment. Not the part about her.

Caiden at least had the good grace to look ashamed. "Fuck," he muttered. His eyes met Zayde's, and they had a whole silent conversation while Winter taped up my thumbs in silence, using way more of the stretchy bandage stuff than was necessary.

Z disappeared from the kitchen, and Cade sighed, rubbing his hand over his face. "It's getting late. Let's talk about it tomorrow, yeah?"

Winter nodded as she examined my thumbs. Satisfied with her work, she released my hands, then leaned up to press a soft kiss to my cheek.

When they'd both left the room, I stayed where I was for a while, my head spinning, before I decided I might as well go upstairs. My thumbs were throbbing, and I needed painkillers. I glared at them. Couldn't even have a fucking wank with them all bandaged up like this.

On the landing, I stopped outside the guest bedroom where Jessa was staying. I lifted my hand to knock but paused when I heard a noise. Pressing my ear to the door, I heard the unmistakable sound of muffled crying coming from inside the room.

There was nothing I could do or say that would make the situation any better. If anything, I'd make it worse.

Lowering my hand, I stepped away.

Her soft cries still echoed in my ears when I closed my bedroom door.

6

jessa

The noises of showers running, people shouting to each other, and slamming doors finally stopped. I waited another ten minutes just to be sure before making my way out of bed. After a quick shower, I threw on another pair of jogging bottoms and a loose navy T-shirt. The T-shirt slipped off my shoulders, and I examined myself in the mirror. I'd lost weight. Too much. But I couldn't bring myself to care.

My stomach growled, and I knew I should eat. I ignored that, too, until it growled again. Winding my damp hair into a ponytail, I grabbed my car keys and handbag. There was no way I was eating here, not when everyone had made it clear how unwelcome I was.

As I headed down the hallway, a crash and the sound of Cassius swearing sounded from somewhere in his room. Without even thinking it through, I stepped up to his door and knocked.

The door swung open, and I was confronted by Cassius wearing nothing but a pair of tight black boxers. My mouth went dry, and I snapped my eyes up to his face, keeping them there with an effort. He frowned down at me, frustration in his gaze, his nostrils flared. "Are you okay?" I ventured.

"No," he said shortly, stepping back and to the side, swinging the door open. I took that as an invitation to enter his room.

"What's the matter?" Leaning against the wall, I glanced around his room. Anything to avoid my gaze straying towards his gorgeous body, so close to me. My eyes barely took in the décor of soft greys and the monstrously oversized bed that dominated the centre of the space before they returned to him. The corners of his lip curved up in amusement, the frustration melting away.

"Take a good look." He spread out his arms. "It's—"

"No." I held up my hand, biting my lip to contain my smile. "Just stop. Tell me what the problem is, and we can discuss your huge ego another time."

"And my huge—"

Lunging forwards, I slammed my hand over his mouth, feeling him laugh under my palm. His fingers came up to curl around my hand, prying it away from his face. "Okay, okay." He shoved his thumbs in front of my face. "This. I need to shave."

Last night in the kitchen...another wave of hurt swamped me, making me catch my breath. I'd almost forgotten about what had happened, what he'd said, too distracted by his presence, but now, everything came flooding back to me. "It wouldn't have happened if you hadn't invited me to stay when I clearly wasn't welcome."

Guilt flared in his eyes, and he lowered his hand. "I didn't mean it like that. You misheard me."

"I know what I heard, Cass." Slumping back against the wall, I sighed. "And I get it. I don't hold it against you, honestly." I'd been awake most of the night, thinking about it, and it was obvious I couldn't stay here much longer, not when it was clear that no one wanted me here. My apartment didn't feel safe, so my plan was to search for a hotel or Airbnb later. It wasn't like I couldn't afford it. I shouldn't have allowed Cassius to talk me into staying in the first place, but I'd been so shaken by the photo that I hadn't been thinking straight.

A low growl came from his throat, and I stared at him, surprised, as his eyes narrowed. "You. Mis. Heard. Me."

"Whatever. Can we not talk about it now, please?" Grasping for anything to change the subject, I pushed off the wall. "Do you want me to help you with shaving?"

"What?"

"I can help. I had to help my brother out when he broke his arm."

He stared at me for a moment, then nodded slowly. "Okay. Thank—" His phone sounded loudly, cutting him off, and I took the opportunity to admire his ass flexing as he walked over to his dresser.

"Fucking wanker," he muttered, frowning at his screen.

"What?"

Turning, he held up his phone, and I stepped closer to view the screen. I had to bite my lip hard to contain my smile. It was a message from Weston with a photo captioned "thumbs up!" The image was of him and Lena, sticking both of their thumbs up. As I stared at it, another message came through beneath the photo. It said, "Shame you can't do this without looking like a twat."

Cassius growled under his breath, stabbing at his phone and replying with a string of middle finger emojis. "Don't start," he warned when I couldn't contain my smile any longer, but before he turned away, I caught his own smile tugging at his lips.

Throwing his phone onto the bed, he turned and headed into his en suite, and I placed my keys and handbag down, then followed him in. The bathroom was in disarray —a can of shaving foam lying on its side in the sink, foam bubbling out of it, the tap left running. A towel was thrown across the floor, and water splashes decorated the tiles. Cassius glanced around the room, subtly winced, then gave me an innocent look, widening his eyes. "What?"

"I didn't say anything." A reluctant smile found its way onto my face again. What was it about Cassius that made me feel lighter after I'd been feeling hopeless for so long?

Now wasn't the time to think about it.

I directed him to sit on the side of the bath while I rinsed the foam out of the sink, then filled the basin with warm water. He tracked my movements with interest, his gaze boring into me, and I shot him a small smile as I turned back from the sink and carefully dampened his skin before applying shaving foam to his jaw.

When I returned with the razor, he'd widened his legs. I paused and then realised that it made sense for me to stand as close to him as possible, so I stepped between them. From this position, I could see the ring of darker blue that ran around his irises. His thick brown lashes were lowered, his gaze on my mouth.

"I didn't mean it about you," he said softly. He raised his head, his eyes meeting mine, and I could see the truth in them. Giving him a nod of assent, I lightly gripped the back of his head, his hair soft beneath my hand.

"Ready?"

He remained silent, so I took that as my cue to begin. I uncapped the razor and began to drag it across his skin, slowly and carefully. The room fell silent, and every tiny sound seemed magnified. The scrape of the razor over stubble, Cassius' breaths close to me, my own breaths, faster than they'd normally be, no matter how unaffected I told myself I was.

Cassius shifted slightly when I lifted the razor away from his skin to check my handiwork, his legs closing, trapping me between his muscular thighs. An involuntary shiver went through my body, and I swallowed, needing moisture for my suddenly dry throat.

"Okay?" he murmured, and I wasn't exactly sure what he was asking me, but I nodded. His hands came up to rest lightly on my hips. "Just steadying you." A familiar grin appeared on his face, but when my eyes met his, there was something else there. Something I wasn't sure I was reading correctly. Either that, or my imagination was running away with me.

Turning my attention back to my task, I decided I *was* imagining things. Until one of the hands resting on my hip slid upwards, under the hem of my T-shirt, and then his fingers were resting on my bare skin.

Every single inch of me zeroed in on that one tiny patch of skin, my nerve endings alight with sensation as his index finger moved almost imperceptibly, stroking up and down. It was too much but not enough. The desire that I thought had died that night at the docks raced through my veins, shocking me with its intensity. My nipples hardened, visible beneath the fabric of my top, and goosebumps popped out along my arms.

What the fuck? Cassius was barely touching me.

With effort, I kept my hand steady, finishing up my task as quickly as possible. Of course it didn't mean anything. This was Cassius. He probably wasn't even aware of what he was doing, the movements instinctual to him.

"I think I'm done." Thankfully, my voice didn't betray me, sounding more or less normal. "I just need to rinse off the razor."

He remained silent, not even looking at me.

When I stepped back, his hands dropped to his thighs, and he cleared his throat. As I turned away, he shifted slightly, and my eyes flashed downwards.

A tiny gasp escaped me, and I immediately slammed my mouth shut.

He was hard.

Not fully hard, but hard enough that it was noticeable. And how strange was it that I was intimately acquainted with the size of Cassius' dick that I instantly knew that information?

My cheeks grew hot, and I stared down at the sink while I dampened a cloth. Overriding everything else I was feeling, though, was that same fizzing excitement I'd had around him before.

I wasn't broken. I could feel again.

Stepping back over to him, careful to avoid his gaze, I cleaned the rest of the shaving foam from his face. His skin was warm and smooth beneath my fingers, and I could feel the flex of his jaw as I slid the cloth over his face.

I took an unsteady breath. "Okay. I'm finished. I'm...I'm going to go now."

"Go where?" His voice came out lower than usual.

"Out. Uh, breakfast. And I'm going to look for a hotel to stay in."

"No." He gripped my arm, his eyes darkening. "You're not going anywhere. You're staying here."

"Why does it matter to you where I stay? We're not exactly friends, Cass."

"Yes, we are." When I raised a brow, he added, "Maybe not close friends, but we *are* friends."

"Even so. Why is it important to you?" I asked quietly, my curiosity getting the better of me.

He was silent for a while, his brow creased in thought. "I feel responsible for you."

My stomach twisted. "I'm not your charity case. And I already have one big brother, I don't need another."

"We're the same age. And..." A glint came into his eye. His grip on my arm loosened, his hand moving lower until he was covering my hand. He slid his fingers between mine, then he tugged my arm forwards suddenly, pressing my hand over the bulge in his boxers.

With a screech, I yanked my hand away, stumbling backwards and hitting the sink. Helpless laughter overtook him, his shoulders shaking, and I gave him a savage glare.

"What the fuck, Cass?"

When he finally managed to control his laughter, he straightened up, meeting my gaze. "Just showing you that our relationship isn't sibling-y." A far too innocent smile appeared on his face.

"Sibling-y isn't a word. But seriously, what the fuck?"

"Don't pretend you didn't like it."

Maybe I did, but that was beside the point. Shaking my head, I turned away from him, moving towards the door. "Bye."

"Wait." He hauled me backwards against his body, his arm coming around my waist. "I'm sorry."

His nearness affected me way more than I was comfortable with right now. "I have to go."

Releasing me, he spun me to face him. "Jessa." His

bright blue eyes were wide and troubled, all his humour wiped away. I instantly missed it.

"It's..." I struggled to articulate my thoughts. "This whole situation is..." My words trailed off.

"Tell me." There was a softness to his voice that I'd never heard before. "Please. I promise I won't say anything to anyone."

His words broke something deep inside, cracking open and exposing me. It was almost a relief to say the words I'd kept hidden for so long. "I'm tired." My eyes filled with tears, my voice wobbling. "Tired of it all."

He reached out to me again, tugging me against him and encircling me in his arms.

The final thread of my composure snapped and I let go, laying my head against his chest and allowing the tears to fall. His hand stroked soothingly up and down my back, through my hair, comforting me as I cried.

"What happened scared me so much. I can't sleep, not without nightmares. I..." My words caught in my throat. "I feel like I'm just going through the motions."

"You haven't been eating properly, have you?"

I shook my head against him. "It's...I haven't been interested."

"You said before that you wanted to get back to normal. You wanted me to treat you normally, yeah?"

Swallowing hard, I whispered against his chest. "Yes."

Pulling back, he gave me a confident smile, his hand still rubbing gently over my back. "In that case, no more talk of leaving. We can't do anything about Littlefinger yet, but I'm not going to let anything happen to you. None of us will. Even if they're not as...happy...about you being here, they've got your back." His eyes flashed, his tone turning harsh. "If Littlefinger dares to try anything, he'll regret ever messing with us."

Something in his absolute certainty gave me hope, and I gave him a tentative smile, blinking my tears away. "I hope you're right."

"I'm always right," he assured me. His eyes swept over me, his gaze assessing, and then he pursed his lips. "Go and get changed into something you feel good in. Or felt good in. We're getting you back to normal. Pack an overnight bag, then text your brother and get us put on the VIP list for his club."

"What?"

A grin curved over his lips. "I'm going to remind you of everything you love. First, I'm taking you out for food. Then we're going to hit London hard, and you're gonna have the best night of your life."

I held his gaze, warring with myself, before I gave in and returned his smile with a small, hesitant one of my own. Cassius...I didn't know what it was exactly, but he seemed to quiet the storm inside my head, to give me hope that I could get through this.

It was time to put my trust in him.

"I'd like that."

7

cassius

The queue for Sanctuary snaked down the street, but we bypassed the line, heading straight up to the door. As soon as Jessa gave the bouncer her name and he realised she was the owner's sister, he was immediately deferential, fawning all over us. Good times.

When we were inside the cavernous main space, a hot as fuck brunette in a short, tight black dress led us across the club, past the long bar, and up to a set of roped-off glass stairs. As we ascended to the upper mezzanine level, she turned, addressing Jessa. "I'm Laura. This is the VIP area. Austin told me to let you know that whatever you want, it's yours. If you need anything, this buzzer on the table will alert myself or one of the other staff."

"Anything?" I questioned, giving her a blatant once-over, letting my lips curve into a smile. Next to me, I heard Jessa sigh.

Laura returned my smile with a sultry one of her own, staring at me from beneath her lashes. "Austin doesn't approve of staff members fraternising with guests, but he doesn't control my free time."

With a smooth move, I extracted my phone from my pocket and handed it to her.

"I finish at three," she told me, inputting her number with one long, midnight blue fingernail. "Hope to hear from you then."

As soon as she was gone, Jessa shook her head at me, pouring champagne from the ice bucket that rested on the table. "Only you. Five minutes in this place, and you've already got someone's number."

I grinned at her. "No one can resist my natural charm." Taking a step closer, I leaned in, right next to her. "Even you," I breathed in her ear, my voice low. At her noticeable shiver, my smile widened, and she shot me a glare, darting back from me.

"Drink your champagne and behave. And don't even think about ditching me as soon as we've arrived."

"As if I would. We're each other's wingman tonight." Picking up my glass, I held it out towards her. "Cheers."

We clinked glasses, and she slid into the booth that circled the table. The VIP area was set on a mezzanine level above the main club, with a series of secluded booths all facing the same direction. The balcony was clear glass, allowing an unobstructed view of the dance floor below. Everything was decorated in shades of black and midnight blue, with burnished gold embellishments that somehow managed to look modern.

My eyes catalogued everything in an instant, then returned to my partner in crime, Jessa, as I slid into the booth next to her.

She looked good. Really fucking good. She'd taken my advice, and she'd worn a short, floaty-type dress in midnight blue. Same colour as the accents in the club, come to think of it. Gold shimmered over her skin, her dark hair hung glossy and straight down her back, and her green eyes were outlined in black and gold, making the green appear even brighter. As she crossed her legs, my eyes were drawn to her smooth, tanned thighs, and I had to grab my drink again to stop myself from reaching out to her. I didn't think she had any idea of the effect she was currently having on me, but she soon would if I didn't focus on why we were here, rather than—

"What's the plan?" Placing her glass down and leaning back against the booth, she glanced over at me, interrupting my thoughts. Her whole body was relaxed, the constant tension she seemed to hold on to nowhere to be found.

Good. That was the way I wanted it. Tonight, we were going to let go and forget all the shit that she was dealing with. This was about reminding Jessa of who she was. A confident, fucking beautiful woman. Who, yeah, maybe had a sharp tongue at times, but that tongue was also extremely talented at giving head—

Fuck. Adjusting myself discreetly, I steered my mind away from that path. "The plan?"

She nodded.

"Finish up this champagne, dance, flirt, see if anyone catches your eye that you want to have fun with..." Trailing off, I gave her a suggestive wink. "Enjoy yourself."

"Okay." Her finger traced the condensation on her glass, a troubled look entering her eyes. "I can do that. I hope."

Scooting closer, I placed my hand lightly on her thigh. I'd removed the bandages on my thumbs just before we'd come out, and it was clear that both Winter and I had been overreacting. Okay, mostly me, not that I'd admit it to anyone. Both cuts had faded to a thin line, and other than some redness around the sides of the cuts and a bit of pain if I pressed down hard on them, they were fine. I let my hand curve around her smooth skin as I met her eyes. "Serious time. If you feel uncomfortable at any point, I'll be here, okay? I'm not gonna go off and leave you."

"What about Laura?" As soon as the words came out, she made a small, distressed noise. "No. That's not...I didn't mean it like that. I just...I want you to have a good time, too, not being stuck with me because you feel like you have to."

Fuck. She was all huge, worried eyes, her shoulders hunched over as her hand clamped around her glass. I had to tread lightly—this was a big deal to her, her first stab at normality, and I needed her to know that what I wanted was to be here for her. Keeping it casual, I shrugged. "Got her number, didn't I? I'll call her later. Or maybe not. But I won't ditch you, I promise. You're going home with me tonight."

"Oh, Cass, are you saying I'm getting lucky later?" Finally, a proper smile appeared, and she batted her lashes at me exaggeratedly.

This, I could deal with. Easily. "I think I'd be the lucky one." Giving her the same deliberate perusal that I'd given Laura earlier, I watched as a flush came over her cheeks, her eyes darkening.

"Stop with your sex voodoo." Her voice came out husky. Shifting, she dropped her head forwards, her hair falling around her face, hiding her expression from me.

"Sex voodoo?"

"You know what I mean," she huffed. Picking up the bottle, she split the remaining champagne between our glasses, a determined look coming into her eyes. "Drink up, and let's do this."

Down on the dance floor, the beat pounded, heavy and hypnotic. Smoke machines turned the air opaque, and lights pulsed in time with the music. Writhing bodies were everywhere, and I curled my arm around Jessa's waist protectively as a guy stumbled into our path, almost sending her flying.

"Okay?" I felt her body tremble against mine, and I tightened my grip on her, leading her to a relatively empty space off to the side of the platform where the DJ stood. She shook her head, and I turned her to face me. "Tell me what it is." I had to dip my head down to her ear to be heard over the music.

Her arms came up to grip my biceps, and she pressed up against me to speak in my ear. "It's just...I'm not used to this anymore." She paused before clarifying, "Being surrounded by so many people. Dancing. Having fun, like I used to." I felt her huff a bitter laugh against my skin. "Stupid, isn't it?"

Winding my arms around her, I pulled her more tightly against me. Our bodies were completely aligned, and my dick was suddenly very, very interested.

For fuck's sake. Now wasn't the time.

"It's not stupid. Let's get you used to it again."

She pulled back slightly, meeting my eyes, and I saw her lips form the word *yes* before she spun in my arms, keeping her body pressed against mine, and began to move to the beat.

Do you know how impossible it is to stop your dick getting hard when a hot woman is sliding her sexy body all over you? I didn't even try to stop it, just let my hands go to her hips, moving us both like we'd done this a hundred times before. As one song merged into the next, I felt her laugh against me, and I lowered my head to her ear. "This good?"

Turning her head slightly, she looked up at me through

her lashes, a slow smile curving across her lips, and that was all the answer I needed. My lips moved from her ear to her neck, not kissing, just moving over her skin. She tilted her head, a clear invitation and one I took full advantage of.

I pressed a kiss to her throat as I ran my hands up her sides, feeling her body shiver against me. Fuck, she smelled so good. Some sexy, spicy kind of perfume that made me think of things that I probably shouldn't be doing with her but really fucking wanted to.

"Is this a private party, or can anyone join?"

Lifting my head, I met the gaze of a gorgeous blonde with a short dress similar to Jessa's, giving us both an appreciative look. Jessa remained pliant in my arms, still moving to the music, and I took my cue from her, leaving the ball in her court. I knew she liked this, or had done, but I wasn't going to push her into anything she wasn't ready for.

"It's up to my girl."

Jessa exhaled against me and extended her slim arm to the blonde, who smiled, letting herself be pulled towards us. She placed her hands on Jessa's hips, just below mine, and together, we began to move. I resumed sliding my lips over Jessa's neck, while Jessa pulled the blonde closer, positioning her so their thighs slid together. Her hands cupped the blonde's ass, and the blonde responded by grinding down on Jessa's thigh while she angled her head to kiss Jessa's jaw.

My cock went from half-mast to rock fucking hard.

The songs merged from one to the next, and our bodies slid together, slow and so fucking sexy. The blonde whispered something in Jessa's ear, and Jessa responded with a small nod, to which the blonde smiled and licked her lips.

Jessa whimpered as one of the blonde's hands left her

hip, dipping between her legs. She moved, leaning forwards and meeting the blonde's lips with her own.

Fuck.

I groaned, pressing harder into Jessa, my cock straining against my jeans as my hands joined hers, cupping the blonde's sexy round ass. They broke apart from their kiss, and then the blonde tilted her head towards mine. Our mouths met, her tongue tangling with mine, while Jessa's head fell back against my shoulder. The blonde's hand continued to move between Jessa's legs as she ground herself against Jessa's thigh, panting into my mouth. Because I was a gentleman, I helped her out by moving my hand between her legs, pushing aside her underwear and sliding two fingers inside her. She moaned into my mouth, writhing on my fingers while she worked her own fingers faster, coming to a shockingly quick climax. Against me, Jessa's body shook as her own orgasm hit her, her body going lax against mine, her breaths coming in fast pants.

"Thanks for that." The blonde stepped back, giving us both an appreciative look as she flicked her hair over her shoulder. "Here." Lifting her hand, she pressed her fingers to my lips. The fingers that had just brought Jessa to orgasm. "Taste your girl."

Obediently, I opened my mouth, sliding my tongue around her digits. "Mmm. That's it." Placing a light kiss to Jessa's lips, she smiled, slow and appreciative. "Thanks for sharing your man with me. See you both around."

Then she was gone.

"What just happened?" Jessa turned, tilting her head to look at me, blinking. "Did that...I didn't dream that, did I?"

"Yeah, you didn't dream it." I flashed her a wide, satisfied grin. Directing her over to the wall, I positioned her to lean against it. "Wait here. Gotta go wash my hands."

She nodded, still looking dazed, flushed from every-thing that had just happened.

Fucking beautiful.

I pressed down on my cock with the heel of my hand, and her eyes darted downwards.

"You didn't—"

"Later."

Turning in the direction of the toilets, I paused, then spun back around. "By the way." I pressed my lips to her ear. "You taste even better than I remember."

8

jessa

You taste even better than I remember.

Cassius' words echoed in my ears as I stood propped up against the wall on shaky legs. What we'd just done...it wasn't that it was a new experience for me, or for Cassius either, for that matter, but it had been so completely unexpected.

Unexpected in the best way. I was coming back into myself, and tonight, the real me had surfaced. The me that had been suppressed ever since the docks.

I loved it.

I knew it wouldn't be that easy, of course. Nothing had been solved yet. But tonight, I could forget about all that. Cassius had somehow known to provide me with exactly what I needed, what I hadn't even known I'd needed.

I didn't want to go back to the old me, though. Not totally. The bitchy side of me, the shallow emptiness that I'd so often felt—that was gone for good, or so I hoped.

My deep thoughts were interrupted by Cassius making his way back over to me. Tall, tattooed, and gorgeous, he drew the eyes of everyone in the vicinity. His dirty-blond hair was artfully dishevelled, his body covered in a ridiculously tight black T-shirt that showed every single bump and groove of his muscles, and dark jeans that looked like they'd been practically sprayed on... My stomach flipped at the sight of him. For once, his gaze didn't stray, remaining on me, and a bright smile appeared on his face as our eyes met.

A rush of *feeling* swept through me—a swirling combination of gratefulness, euphoria, and heady, heady lust. I trembled with the sudden need to touch him, my senses overwhelmed as he came to a stop right in front of me. Never breaking eye contact, he lifted his hand and brushed a strand of hair away from my face, sending a shiver through my body.

I wanted him.

I wanted him so, so much.

"Hi," he said.

In reply, I closed the last few millimetres of distance between us. His sudden exhale hit my lips, and then his mouth came down on mine.

Maybe it was the fact that this was the first man I'd kissed in months, or maybe it was his skilful mouth, but this kiss was like nothing else. It was incomparable.

His tongue licked into my mouth, one hand gripping the back of my head while the other ran down my back and onto my ass, tugging me against him. I lost myself in him, his body hot against mine, my hands in his hair, then my nails scraping over the back of his neck.

"This probably isn't a good idea." His mouth moved to my throat, kissing and licking his way down to my collarbone.

Grabbing a handful of his hair, I pulled so he'd look up

at me, smirking at his sudden screech. "Do you want to stop?"

"Fuck, no. I love bad ideas." He dived for my mouth again, and I smiled against his lips.

This. This was what I needed.

When he ran his hand over my body, stopping on one of my breasts, I moaned, lifting my head. "Cass."

"Yeah?"

"Want to go back to the hotel?"

In reply, he grabbed my hand and led me in the direction of the exit.

Out on the street, he pressed me against the wall next to the club, sliding his mouth over mine again. I could feel his hardness against me, and I reached down between us to palm his length.

"I want you." His voice was strained. "My cock really isn't happy being confined like this."

A laugh escaped me, despite the haze of lust. He continued talking, dragging my body against his. "I've spent the last however long with you grinding all over my dick, had to feel you coming against me, and I haven't had any action yet."

"Aw, are you feeling neglected?" I slid my hands up his back, feeling his muscles flex beneath the cotton of his T-shirt. Pressing a kiss to his jaw, I smiled. "Mmm. Your jaw's so smooth. Whoever shaved you must've been incredibly talented."

He breathed out a half laugh, half groan against the side of my face. "Yeah." Tugging me away from the wall, he led us in the direction of the hotel at a fast pace. Luckily, it wasn't far. We had separate rooms, but I had a feeling we'd only be seeing the inside of one of them.

"You said incredibly talented?" He shot me a blazing look. "I'll tell you what else you're incredibly talented at." We stepped inside the hotel lobby, quiet except for the night porter. Coming to a stop in front of the lifts, he hit the button, and the doors opened straight away. After pressing the button for our floor, he crowded me into the corner of the lift. Dipping his head, he took my lobe between his teeth before releasing.

"What else am I incredibly talented at?" I asked breathlessly, arching against him as his teeth ran down my neck. I fucking loved it when he was like this. Loved his playful side, too, but this sexy, predatory side of him...it set me on fire.

Gripping my hand, he pushed it down between us, over the hard bulge in his jeans. His voice was a low growl against my throat. "Sucking. My. Cock."

"*Yes.*"

We stumbled out of the lift, barely separating to get the key card in the door of Cassius' room. The second the door slammed shut behind us, Cassius was on me, stripping me out of my dress and underwear, leaving me bared to him.

"Fuck." He stepped back, swallowing hard, his hands working at his jeans as he gave me another searing look. The bright blue of his eyes was almost swallowed by his pupils. "You look even better than I remember."

His words were reminiscent of those he'd said earlier, and they sent a jolt of lust through me. "Have you even seen me like this?" Stalking over to him, I slid my hands down his body and gripped the hem of his T-shirt, tugging it up. "Because I haven't seen all of you yet. And I want to."

He gave a kind of choked moan as I freed him of his T-shirt. We'd slept together once before, a long time ago, and we'd fooled around on quite a few occasions, although not for a long time now. It had always been meaningless fun, another way to let go and live in the moment without worry. We'd never bared ourselves to each other before, though—literally or figuratively. Dropping to my knees, I peeled his jeans down, which wasn't easy since they were so tight. But the reward was so worth it. When he finally stepped out of them, I ran my hands up his strong calves, up the back of his thighs, and onto his ass.

"So sexy," I murmured, gripping him and pulling his hips forwards. I stared up at him from beneath my lashes as I closed my lips around the head of his cock, straining at the fabric of his underwear. When I lifted my head, his hands came to my hair, roughly caressing the strands, his lids lowering as he looked down at me.

"Suck me, Jessa. I wanna fuck that pretty mouth."

His usual teasing tone was absent, his gaze full of fire, and I eased down his underwear, taking his thick length in my hand. "You want me to suck your cock, huh?" Dipping down, I flicked my tongue over the head with the barest pressure, making him groan.

"Babe, you're *killing* me."

"So impatient." I moved my head lower, licking a long, slow stripe from the base all the way to the tip while I lightly cupped his balls. Glancing back up at him, I saw his lids had lowered, his lashes hiding his expression from me. He was sucking his bottom lip between his teeth, his stomach muscles tensed. Fuck, he was so close to the edge already. I didn't want him to come yet, though.

Rising up higher, I kept my grip on his cock, stroking him up and down so, so slowly. A hiss escaped from between his teeth, and he tried to thrust into my hand, but I kept my grip loose. I pressed a kiss to his abs, then licked and kissed down the slope of his V, repeating the process on the other side. His body was a work of art, and I'd never had the chance to explore it in detail before.

His hands tightened their grip in my hair, tugging slightly, and I smiled, pressing one final kiss to his skin before raising my head. He'd been patient enough, and we both needed this. "*Now* you can fuck my mouth."

Then I lowered my head, wrapped my lips around him, and opened my throat, taking almost his entire hard length in one long movement, despite his size.

"Fuuuck." His strangled groan was accompanied by his hips thrusting forwards, and I moaned around his cock as he fucked into my mouth, angling my head forwards until there was no possible way I could fit any more of him inside me. My vision blurred with tears, and my lungs burned, and I pulled back to take a breath, switching things up by dragging my tongue over his sensitive head while my hand played with his balls and taint. He groaned again, his head falling back against the wall behind him as I swallowed his cock again, hollowing my cheeks as I hummed around his thick length. His hips thrust forwards, and his legs tensed against me. Without warning, he pulled out of my mouth, and then his cum was hitting my mouth, my face, and my body.

"Fucking *fuck*." He slumped back against the wall, his eyes closed, and let himself slide down to the floor.

When he opened his eyes, I gave him a satisfied smile. "Good?" My voice came out raspy, thanks to the way he'd been fucking my throat.

"Jessa...fuuuuck. Better than good." His gaze tracked over me, and he leaned forwards to pull me onto his lap. "Look at you, all covered in cum." Reaching out, he traced my bottom lip with his finger before lightly pushing it against my closed mouth. I took the hint and opened for him, my tongue sliding over his finger and tasting the salty tang before he removed his finger and kissed me.

"Cass," I moaned as he trailed kisses down my throat. "I want..."

"What do you want, babe?"

Pulling back, I met his gaze, all heavy-lidded and sexy. "You inside me."

"It's like you read my mind." A slow, teasing smile curved over his lips. "Gimme five minutes to recover, and I'll blow your mind."

I shot him a look, even as my heart rate sped up. "Five minutes? And these are big promises you're making."

He nipped at my bottom lip, his hands coming up to caress my breasts, making my breath catch in my throat. "My recovery time is legendary. And I never promise things I can't deliver."

"Well..." I arched into his touch. "I need to clean up, because someone thought this was a good idea." Waving a hand at myself, I caught his satisfied smirk. "Want to check the water pressure in the shower with me?"

Lifting me from his lap, he rose to his feet, extending his hand to me. "I was about to suggest the same thing."

We didn't make it to the bed.

Maybe his five minutes recovery time was an exaggeration, but I wasn't counting. As soon as he began soaping my body, his dick was lengthening, and by the time he'd dipped his fingers between my legs, he was fully hard, grinding against my ass. His hot breath hit my ear, water streaking off his head and down over my body. "It was so fucking hot feeling you come against me while that girl touched you. But I want to feel you come all over my fingers now. Are you gonna come for me, babe?"

I moaned, tipping my head to the side, my senses overloaded by everywhere he was touching me—his teeth nipping at my throat, his hands working over my breasts, my clit, and his fingers curling inside me. It had been fun earlier in the club, but this, right now...it didn't even compare.

"That's it. Come for me." He increased the pressure, and I fell apart, riding the wave of my orgasm, head thrown back against his shoulder and my body braced against his, holding me up.

When I recovered, coming back to myself, he spun me gently to face him. There was a wide grin on his face that just radiated smugness. I raised a brow, doing my best to ignore the way the water was falling over his hard body, although I couldn't help my gaze flicking downwards, cataloguing his dips and lines, and the thick length of his cock jutting out between us, brushing against my hip.

So gorgeous.

My breaths came faster, but I kept my voice level. "What?"

"I made you come on command." The smugness increased as he spoke, and I shook my head. How could I be irritated, amused, and completely and utterly turned on all at once?

"That was a coincidence," I told him, but he shook his head.

"It's part of my sex voodoo powers."

"Never say you have sex voodoo powers again."

"I make no promises. Anyway, you said it to me first."

My smile matched his, but as much as I could banter with him all day, we had way more important things to do. Things that involved him being inside me, preferably as soon as possible. Stepping closer, I placed my palms flat against his chest, feeling his increasing heart rate under my palm. Sliding them lower, I tilted my head up to his at the same time his mouth came down on mine.

And that was when Cassius Drummond took control.

I barely had a chance to move my hands away and wrap my arms around his neck before he was scooping me up, lifting me up against the shower wall, his mouth covering mine, and then he was angling my body and sliding me down onto his hard length.

My grip on him tightened, my arms and legs wrapped around him as he pounded into me, the angle so perfect that I knew I wouldn't last long before I was coming all over his cock. I was so full, so overwhelmed by this man who knew exactly how to play my body, like it was made for him.

"Cass." A moan fell from my lips as he latched onto my throat, sucking a mark into my skin.

"Come for me, baby," he said in a low, commanding voice, and I shattered around him, swept away on a high I never wanted to come down from. Pumping his hips harder, he growled against my throat, raw and animalistic, and then his cock was pulsing inside me, filling me with his cum.

His cum.

"Cass!" The horror in my tone wiped the lustful pleasure from his face so fast, I reeled backwards.

"What?"

"We didn't use a condom!" My breaths were coming in shallow pants, panic probably written all over my face.

"Oh." Giving another couple of lazy pumps of his hips, he leaned forwards and placed a kiss to the corner of my mouth.

"What do you mean, *oh*? This is serious."

Lifting me off him, he directed me under the stream of

water still pouring from the giant showerhead. "I take my responsibilities as a sex voo—sex god very seriously, Jessa."

"Sex god—what? What's that even supposed to mean?"

"It means that I make sure I get regularly tested, since I have sex god responsibilities to fulfil." He flashed me a grin. "And I never, ever fuck anyone without a condom."

"Except you just did," I pointed out, my heart rate slowly coming down as his words penetrated the fog of panic that had overtaken my mind.

"Except I just did," he repeated slowly. Sucking his bottom lip between his teeth, he studied me with an inscrutable expression. "I guess we got caught up in the moment, yeah?"

I shrugged, tipping my head back to let the water cascade down my back. Cassius reached over to my left and handed me a washcloth that he drizzled shower gel on.

"You're protected, right? And you've been tested or whatever?"

I moved the washcloth over my body in small circles, holding eye contact with him. His gaze was confident, unconcerned, and the last of my panic died away. "Yeah. I just... It was a shock."

Placing his hand on my shoulders, he turned me. "Then we don't have anything to stress about. Here. Let me do your back." I handed him the washcloth, the moment so normal, so familiar, that it took me aback. Closing my eyes, I breathed in and out deeply.

"That's twice now." Cassius' voice was suddenly right by my ear, making my eyes fly open.

"Twice what?"

"Twice that I've made you come on command."

"Does this man have any limits to his ego?" I wondered aloud. Then, turning my head, I treated him to an eye roll.

"Pure coincidence, both times." I left out the whole thing about him knowing how to play my body perfectly—he did not need that kind of information to inflate his already huge ego.

He shook his head, disbelieving. "Don't even pretend that you didn't love every second of what happened tonight."

I turned to face him fully, linking my arms around his neck, because whatever he might say to me, how could I resist a gorgeous, naked, wet Cassius Drummond? "Mmm. I could probably be persuaded to go for another round, if your legendary recovery skills are up to the job."

A gleam came into his eye. "Is that a challenge?" Without breaking eye contact, he reached over and turned the shower off. "Bed. Now."

9

jessa

Cassius was still asleep when I woke the next morning. Sprawled out on the huge bed on his stomach, his tanned skin golden against the crisp white sheets, he was beautiful. I'd known I'd have a good time with him, but last night had been something else.

I stretched, deliciously sore. After the shower, we'd fucked against the window and again in the bed, and then both of us had succumbed to exhaustion sometime after the sun had already risen in the sky.

Sitting up, I pushed my tangle of hair back from my eyes. Cassius had known exactly what I needed. This whole overnight trip had reset something inside me. While the fear and pain remained at the back of my mind, I now felt more able to handle it. Stronger, somehow. I had a lot to be grateful for.

By the time Cassius woke, I was showered and dressed, having retrieved my bag from my own hotel room, and was in the middle of a text conversation with Austin, who was grilling me on my experience in Sanctuary. It was a shame he hadn't been around to meet up with us, but at the same time, it was probably a good thing. I could just imagine him pulling the overprotective older brother act with Cassius, even though there was nothing between us—other than a night of incredibly hot sex, *not* that my brother would be privy to that kind of information. In fact, now that I thought about it, it was a really, really good thing he hadn't been at the club last night. What Cassius and I had done with the blonde girl, right on the dance floor... I shuddered, grimacing. There were some things that a sibling should never, ever see.

"Morning." Cassius twisted to look across at where I was sitting on the sofa, shading his eyes against the sunlight streaming through the huge windows.

"Hi." I smiled at him. "Coffee?"

He nodded, stifling a yawn, before scrubbing his hand over his tousled hair. "Please. What's the time?"

"Almost ten." Standing, I picked up the coffee I'd purchased earlier and moved to the bed. Sinking down onto the mattress, I handed it to him. "It should still be warm."

Pushing himself into a seated position, he leaned back against the headboard. "This isn't the hotel coffee." He examined the cup, a pleased smile curving over his lips.

"I went to the coffee place next door. I was dying for a double shot of espresso in my latte, and I remembered that you had a weird thing about hotel coffee."

He flicked me an appreciative look. "Thanks." As he tipped the coffee to his lips, a groan came from his throat that was way too sexy for this time of the morning. Especially after three hours' sleep, when my body needed time to recover from what we'd put it through.

Shifting on the bed, I redirected my thoughts away from the undeniable effect he had on my libido. "Cass?"

Sensing the seriousness of my tone, he gave me his full attention. "What's up?"

"I just wanted to say thanks for all this. It was just what I needed."

"I know it was." For once, his eyes held no humour, and his voice was soft. "Are you ready to face the world again now?"

"I don't know," I said honestly, "but I feel like I might be able to."

"Good." Reaching out, he laid his hand over mine for a brief moment before pulling away. "Guess we'd better burst this sex bubble and go back to reality, huh? Unless you feel like another round before we check out?" Tugging the sheet lower on his hips, he shot me a filthy look, biting at his lip and staring at me from beneath his thick lashes.

Heat raced through me, my body instantly responding to him. Sucking in a breath, I closed my eyes. "I want to, but I think you broke me. I need time to recover." Opening my eyes again, I placed my hand on his thigh and gave him a slow smile. "I suppose I am feeling thankful enough to reward you, though."

I yanked off the sheet, lowered my body to the bed, and wrapped my lips around his cock.

Three hours later, I'd have given anything to be back in that hotel room. Anything was better than having the full attention of the Four on me, their looks ranging from disapproval to hostility. Caiden had noticed my new neck decoration, aka the purpling bruise on my throat, courtesy of Mr. Drummond, and he kept shooting Cassius wounded looks, as if he was personally betrayed by the sight.

Ignoring him, I placed the photo down on the lounge coffee table, pointing out the objects with a clinical detachment. If I concentrated on the facts, and even how uncomfortable I was, then the fear couldn't break through.

"This is from my kidnapper. The rope and the material, th-that—" To my horror, my voice cracked. I couldn't even get through *one fucking sentence* without breaking down?

A hand came down over mine and gently squeezed. I glanced up in surprise to see Winter had moved to perch on the arm of my sofa. Shooting her a grateful smile, I swallowed hard, managing to get the rest of the sentence out. "That was what they used to tie me up and gag me with." Darkness flashed in my mind, but before it could pull me under, I looked straight across at Cassius, who was watching me intently, and I let memories of last night wash over me instead. His stare turned heated, as if he could read every dirty image that was playing through my head.

I shifted in my seat.

"What about the pointy metal thing?" Winter gave my hand another squeeze, drawing my attention back to the image. "And the blood? I think it's blood?" She wrinkled her nose.

"I stabbed him with it." My voice came out as a whisper, but everyone heard me. Zayde stared at me with new interest in his icy eyes, and Weston raised a brow.

Cassius leaned forwards. "Where did you stab him?"

"Do you feel like telling us what happened?" Lena spoke up at the same time, eyeing me with empathy in her blue eyes. Out of everyone, she was the person I felt most comfortable with, other than Cassius. She gave me a small, encouraging smile, and I nodded. The last thing I wanted to do was relive the experience again—it happened enough in my nightmares, but maybe this would help to explain to everyone why I'd been so shaken. Why I'd come here, despite knowing that I wasn't exactly welcome.

Taking a deep breath, I began.

When I'd finished, the silence in the room was absolute.

Caiden met my eyes, his face an impenetrable mask, but he swallowed hard, his throat working. "Fuck. I think I speak for us all when I say we'll give you our full support." He paused, and his gaze flicked to Winter before it returned to me. "You're welcome to stay with us for as long as you need."

"Thank you," I told him, and I meant it.

"Can we answer my question now? Where did you stab him?" Cassius shot me a reassuring grin. "Did you know that Winter's nickname was Stabby for a while? We might have to pass the nickname on to you."

"Please don't." I gave him a warning look, biting the inside of my cheek to stop my smile. "As for where I stabbed him, I really don't know. It was all a blur." Thinking hard, I replayed the moment in my mind. The cold rain, the feel of the metal in my hand, the ease with which it pierced through denim and flesh. "I was on the ground, right by his legs, and I kind of jabbed upwards." I mimicked the motion with my hand.

"Like this?" Cassius gripped Weston's arm, pulling him to his feet, then dropped to the floor. In one quick move, he punched upwards.

Straight into Weston's balls.

"You fucker!" West dropped down, clutching himself. "Fucking *fuck*!"

"That'll teach you not to take the piss out of my injuries." Cassius grinned in satisfaction.

"Mate! Your fucking thumbs were bandaged. You looked ridiculous. You don't go around punching your best friend in his most sensitive area as payback." Groaning, he glared over at Cassius from his prone position on the floor. "Do you want to ruin your chances of becoming an uncle one day?"

"Yeah. What happened to your whole 'I'm a lover, not a fighter' philosophy?" Winter interjected.

"Babe, you're supposed to be on my side." Cassius gave her a mock-wounded look, sticking out his bottom lip, and that was the moment that I started laughing uncontrollably.

It was cathartic, like I was shedding a heavy burden. As they continued to banter around me, my laughter came to a stop, and I sank back in my chair.

This right here. This was what it was like to be around people that cared about each other. The unbreakable bond of this family that had each other's backs no matter what and understood each other so well.

Something I'd never known before.

I *ached* for it.

Cassius glanced over at me, and all my defences were down, and I knew that he could see everything I was feeling right then. Clambering to his feet, he closed the distance between us and dropped an unexpected kiss on the top of my head, squeezing the back of my neck gently. I stilled, feeling a flush stealing over my cheeks. Although I was grateful for everything he'd done for me, and I probably wouldn't ever be able to repay him, I didn't want him to feel like he had to be there for me out of some sense of obligation or whatever was driving him to act this way.

He spoke from beside me, addressing the room. "I've decided we're calling this Operation Littlefinger. We need a theme tune."

"A theme tune?" Winter stared up at him, and I heard "for fuck's sake" muttered from Zayde's direction.

"Yeah. Like we did with Operation Andromeda."

"We did not have a theme tune." Weston shook his head. "But I like this idea. Wanna see my playlist? There's a couple of..."

I tuned out his voice as Winter leaned her head close to mine. "They could be here a while. May as well get comfortable. Do you want a drink?"

"Please."

Following her into the kitchen, I leaned against the marble island. "I should have said this sooner, but I really am sorry for the way I acted towards you when you came to Alstone. I was...jealous. I don't know what I can say to make it right, but if I could go back and change things, I would."

She smiled. "Thank you. I know I said that I wasn't sure if we'd ever be friends, but I'm beginning to see that I might be wrong about that. Maybe we could do something together? If you feel happy about it, with everything else that's going on. What do you like to do?"

My mouth twisted. "My life's not exactly filled with exciting pursuits. I like...or liked, I guess...partying, hanging out at the beach, reading, and...I suppose that's about it."

Winter stared at me thoughtfully. "You make it sound like a bad thing. Look, I know for a fact that you work really hard in your degree course, and you're being prepped to work for the family business. Just like I am now, I guess. So you're perfectly entitled to relax and have fun doing whatever you want to do in your free time. I feel like once we graduate, we're going to have even less free time, so we should make the most of it while we can."

I relaxed at her words. "You're right. Okay...well, while we don't know where Petr is, I'm not sure how comfortable

I'd feel about going out and about. The fact he knows where I live...that really shook me."

"So...what if we go to your brother's club again? I've never been to a London club, and the security will be tight, won't it?" Her voice grew more excited. "I bet we could get Creed to do us a deal on hotel rooms, too."

"Creed? Ooh, yes. I don't know him, but my brother works with him now," I told her.

"Even better." Turning to the fridge, she opened it and stared inside. "Pear cider okay?"

"As long as it's cold, I'll take it."

We ended up sitting outside on the deck, and one by one, the others drifted out to join us. All of them. Something between us had shifted, and I felt like they'd allowed me a tiny glimpse into their tightly knit circle today.

As the sky grew dark outside and the deck grew smoky with the scent of weed heavy in the air, I stretched, curling my legs up under me. Cassius caught my eye from across the deck, where he'd been in conversation with Weston.

When his bright blue eyes met mine and his lips curved into a smile, my heart skipped a beat, and butterflies fluttered in my stomach.

I sucked in a shocked breath, my eyes widening at the realisation.

No. *No*.

Sex was one thing, but I *couldn't* catch feelings for Cassius Drummond. The biggest player I knew, the man who claimed he liked to share the love, the man for whom "commitment" was a dirty word.

I'd always been on board with the whole sharing the love thing, and we'd messed around and slept together in the past without either of us expecting or wanting anything more. What had changed now, and why had it suddenly snuck up on me at the worst possible moment, with the one man that I shouldn't and couldn't have?

I needed to shut this down right now—falling for him was the worst thing I could do. That was a one-way ticket to heartbreak.

As I helplessly returned his smile, though, I had a sinking feeling it was already too late.

10

cassius

Three days later, I woke up in a great mood, even though it was way, way too early to be up. The birds hadn't even started making noise outside my window when I'd rolled out of bed. But we finally had a lead on Petr. West had managed to track him down at some dive hotel in London, which meant that at least he wasn't staying in the local area—a fact Jessa seemed grateful for.

Whistling, I wandered into the kitchen and threw on my apron. We'd need a big breakfast to be ready for today.

"West. You're on egg duty. I'm doing bacon."

"Why do you have to cook bacon naked?" Lena whined. "My own brother. It's sickening."

"There's nothing sickening about this body. Isn't that right, Jessa?"

Jessa stopped dead in the kitchen doorway, blinking the sleep out of her eyes. As she turned to me, her eyes widened. I watched in satisfaction as her cheeks flushed. Her mouth opened and closed, and then her gaze smoothed out, becoming unreadable. "Nope, nothing sickening at all." She strolled over to the island and gracefully swung herself onto one of the stools. The silky pale blue material of her shorts rode up as she crossed one long tanned leg over the other. "Do you need me to help? If not, I'll sit right here and enjoy the view."

"I'll be in the computer room until breakfast is ready," Lena announced, backing out of the kitchen.

"You sit there and look pretty." Stopping next to Jessa, I trailed my hand down her back. "Makes a change to look at something other than West's ugly mug."

"Ugly. Please." Weston rolled his eyes. "Feel privileged, Jessa. Cass doesn't cook breakfast for his other one-night stands."

There was a crash as I dropped the pan I was holding, and I shot my best mate a savage glare. "Jessa's a guest here. Not a one-night stand." I straightened up from picking the pan up in time to see West giving Jessa's neck a pointed glance. Moving around her, I lifted my hand and brushed my thumb over where I'd marked her. Fuck knows what had possessed me to do that. It wasn't something I normally did. More like the kind of thing possessive guys like Cade did, trying to be all alpha and visually claim their woman or some shit. Since I didn't have an explanation other than being caught up in the moment, I played it off. "What can I say? Jessa has a vampire fetish. Sadly, it turns out that my teeth are too blunt, and I don't like the taste of blood."

Jessa huffed out an amused laugh. "I have a vampire fetish, do I?"

"That's what you told me." I gave her an innocent smile, which I then directed at West. He shook his head as he cracked eggs into a pan. "Your girlfriend used to kiss a poster of Edward Cullen every night before bed," I added, knowing that would redirect his thoughts.

He recoiled with a look of disgust. "That better not be true." Abandoning the eggs, he rushed out of the kitchen, and I laughed as I heard him call Lena's name.

"Is it true?" Jessa swung off the stool and moved around to the other side of the island, taking up Weston's job of cracking the eggs.

"Nah, but it's fun to wind them up sometimes."

A wistful expression flitted over her face before it was gone. "You get on well with Lena, don't you?"

"Yeah. She's a pain in my ass sometimes, the way she goes rushing into shit without thinking of the consequences, but I wouldn't change her." I turned away from Jessa to lay the strips of bacon in the pan. "Wanna bring the eggs over?"

When she was standing next to me at the range cooker, prodding at the slowly scrambling eggs, I picked up the thread of our conversation. "Do you get on alright with your brother?"

"I do. I guess...it's different. He's my half-brother, not that it makes a difference, but he's always been quite independent. Kind of aloof, I guess you could say. When he was eighteen, he moved out to live with friends in London, and he started building up his business. I was only fourteen at the time. I always looked up to him, though, and I know he'd do anything for me if I asked. He's constantly busy, but he always sets aside time to see me and calls and texts me, stuff like that."

Turning the bacon, careful of the hiss of hot fat from the pan, I asked the question I was most curious about. "Does he know about what happened at the docks?"

She shook her head violently. "No, and that's the way it's going to stay." There was a long pause, and then she added with a sigh, "Unless it becomes unavoidable now that Petr is here."

Her voice was so sad that I put down the spatula I was holding and pulled her into my arms. She sighed again, her breath skating across my collarbone. "Cass."

"Yeah?"

"As nice as this is, it's kind of weird being hugged by someone who's naked other than wearing an apron."

"I wouldn't know. Wanna get naked so I can tell you how it feels?"

Her hand slapped my bare ass. "Behave."

"Excuse me?" Just for that ass slap, I groped hers. My dick stirred, enjoying the feel of her fucking hot body way too much, and I quickly released her, stepping back. A hard-on wasn't a great idea when you were only wearing an apron and cooking hot food. "No bacon boners," I muttered to myself, earning a raised brow from Jessa.

"I'm not even going to ask what that means."

"Best not to," I agreed, examining the bacon. "Bacon's ready. How are the eggs?"

She turned off the hob and gave the pan a small shake. "Done."

When everyone was assembled in the kitchen, devouring the piles of food, we went through our plan. After all the shit that had gone down in the past, it was a simple one: find Petr and ask him what the fuck he was doing. I wasn't sure how the asking part was going to go down, but I had an idea, thanks to the look of bloodthirsty excitement Cade and Z were both trying and failing to conceal. As far as I was concerned, anything that would get this situation sorted out soonest was good with me. None of us were expecting much trouble—we'd established that Petr was acting alone, and really, what could one man do?

Cade, Z, and I were taking my SUV while West and Lena were on standby for any computer shit that needed doing. Jessa...she hid it well, but I think everything that had happened had fucked with her head more than she let on, so I'd pulled Winter aside and asked her to distract Jessa today while we were otherwise occupied.

So anyway, that was our plan. Breakfast done, the three of us piled into my SUV, escaping while Jessa was in the shower. We arrived in London just before 8:30 a.m., and I managed to sneak into a street parking spot close to the hotel Littlefinger was staying in.

"What the fuck kind of dive is this?" Cade stared at the peeling, chipped front door, covered in a faded red plastic awning that said "Queen's Hotel."

"The kind that has a one-star rating on TripAdvisor." I stepped across the broken tiles outside the door and pushed it open a crack, peering inside. There was a bored-looking brunette at the front desk, playing with her phone. Other than that, the area was empty. Closing the door again, I lowered my voice. "Operation Littlefinger has commenced. I'll distract the woman in reception while you two sneak past."

"Alright. You sure?"

"Yeah." I nodded at Cade. "I'm more charming than you, and Z would probably make her cry with his serial killer stare." Zayde directed said stare at me, and I stared right back, unimpressed. "That look doesn't work on me, mate. I'm immune."

Narrowing his eyes at me, he increased the intensity of his glare, and I widened my eyes. "Cade, he wants to kill me!"

"Shut the fuck up, you idiot." Caiden cuffed me round the back of my head, and I cuffed him right back.

Zayde rolled his eyes at us, tapping a non-existent watch on his wrist. "Are you two finished?"

"N—" I caught Cade's eye. "Yes." He smirked at me, and I gave him a wide, fake grin as I pushed the front door open all the way and headed inside. The receptionist raised her head when I entered, and I immediately dialled up my smile, crossing over to the desk. I positioned myself at the side so she'd have to turn away from the door and stairs to view me and leaned my arms on the desk, making sure I flexed my biceps.

Of course, she couldn't resist my charm. Crowding into my personal space, she leaned right over the desk, not so subtly tugging the neckline of her top down so I could get a better view of her cleavage. I appreciated the effort.

"Are you lost?" She looked me up and down.

She'd given me an opening, and I might as well run with it. "Yes. I am looking for...how you say...Buck-ing-ham Palace?" For some reason, I'd affected an unidentifiable accent.

"I thought so. We don't get men that look like you checking in here."

"What...you mean?" Fuck. My accent had managed to change again, but luckily, she didn't seem to notice, too busy undressing me with her eyes.

Her hand slid onto my bicep, and she gave it a squeeze. "Handsome. Rich."

"I am both of those things." Out of the corner of my eye, I noticed that Caiden and Zayde had disappeared up the top of the stairs, and I let myself relax. Now, I just had to keep up the flirting until they came back. And try to stick to one accent.

Batting her lashes at me, she gave my bicep one last squeeze before she released her grip and opened a drawer at the side of the desk. "I'm assuming that from your question, you don't have a maps app on your phone?"

I shook my head, sticking out my bottom lip sadly, and she melted. "Don't you worry. I'll sort you out." She began unfolding a map that, by the time it was fully unfolded, took up almost the entire reception desk. "Now, see. We're here..." Grabbing a biro, she circled an area on the map, then circled it another three times, just in case I didn't get it. "You want to go down here..." Drawing a wobbly line on the map, she described where I needed to go, and I made affirmative noises every now and then, while keeping one eye on the stairs. When she'd finished explaining and there was still no sign of my friends, I kept her occupied, asking her for bar and restaurant recommendations.

Fucking finally, Cade and Z appeared at the top of the stairs, and I amped up the flirting with a few more muscle flexes and more smiles until they were safely outside. At that point, I made my excuses to leave, leaning over and planting a kiss on her cheek as a thank-you. She pressed a hotel business card into my hand, which she'd scribbled on, and handed me the unfolded map. "You have my personal number there. Enjoy Buckingham Palace."

I blew her a kiss as I exited, then stopped outside the front door to fold the map up. The fucking thing wouldn't fold properly, but eventually I managed to wrestle it into submission, ignoring Cade smirking at me yet again.

"Any luck?" I got straight to the point.

Cade shrugged as we set off in the direction of my car. "Yes and no." He handed me his phone, open to the photo gallery, and I scrolled through the images. "The room was easy enough to get into, but he wasn't there, and there wasn't much of interest. But..." He paused, and a note of hesitation entered his voice. "We did find this phone number written on a scrap of paper, which took West a bit of time to trace."

"What's up with the number?" A weird feeling of foreboding came over me.

"It's the number for a phone extension in Creed's offices."

"The fuck?"

"That's not all." Cade ran his hand through his dark hair, clearly agitated. He flicked his gaze to Zayde, then back to me. "The number belongs to Austin De Witt. Jessa's brother."

11

cassius

"Mr. Pope is out of town until the weekend."

Thanks to Z's connections and his all-access black card, we'd made it into the inner sanctum of Creed's private offices and were now standing in front of a large desk where a gorgeous woman with wavy blue hair sat, eyeing us.

"Natalie, is it?" I leaned over the desk, giving her a wide grin. She smiled and blushed but gave a small eye roll.

"You're Cassius Drummond."

"I am. How did you know?"

"Your reputation precedes you," she said dryly, and I wasn't sure if that was a compliment or not, but I decided to take it as one.

"Did you hear that, Cade?" I elbowed him in the side. "I'm infamous." Caiden rudely ignored me, speaking to Natalie instead.

"Can you set up a meeting when he's back?"

I noticed Zayde was pointedly ignoring Natalie, and her gaze kept darting to him. I made a note to get the details out of him later and returned my attention to Natalie, who was now tapping at her computer.

"The earliest I can fit you in is next Wednesday at two. Does that work?"

Zayde made some kind of disgruntled sound. "Forget it, I'll set it up." He pulled his phone from his pocket and spun on his heel, heading over to the windows.

"Do you know Austin De Witt?" I figured we might as well get some information from her while we were here.

She paused in her typing to glance up at me. "Of course. Why, what do you want to know?"

Has he had any meetings with any suspicious-looking Belarusian guys with part of a finger missing?

"What do you think of him?"

Her eyes narrowed. "He's a trusted colleague of Mr. Pope."

Right.

"Cass." Caiden shook his head at me, and I dropped it. Zayde took that moment to come back over, tilting his head to indicate the exit.

"Sorted it." He began to walk away without a backwards glance. Guess we were done here. I smiled at Natalie again.

"Thanks for all your help, beautiful."

She returned my smile, this time giving me her full attention. I watched in satisfaction as her pupils dilated. "If you need any more help with anything, here's my number." Sliding a business card across the desk to me, she gave me a look that let me know exactly the kind of help she was thinking of, as if it wasn't already obvious. I pocketed the card with a grin and followed the others into the lift.

As soon as the doors closed behind us, I turned to Zayde. "What's the story with the sexy secretary?"

He rolled his eyes. "No story. We had a one-night thing, she wanted a repeat, I didn't. She took it personally."

I stared at him with new respect. "Wow. If she wanted a repeat with *you* that badly, then your dick must've been memorable. Wanna threesome? I need to see these skills in action."

"Fuck off."

"Your loss."

The corners of his mouth lifted in amusement, and he leaned against the wall of the lift, folding his arms across his chest. "Enough of that. Creed's meeting us Saturday night."

"What are we doing about Austin?" I glanced between them both, and Caiden shrugged.

"You don't want to do anything about him 'til you've spoken to Jessa, yeah?" Zayde waited until I nodded, then continued. "Good. We're meeting Creed at Sanctuary."

"Aren't you a sight for sore eyes?" I pulled Winter into a hug, spinning her around so her glossy hair flew around her, and she laughed.

"I take it you like the new hair?"

Putting her down, I ran my fingers through the strands. Still long and dark, but now her hair was threaded through with subtle lighter tones. Yeah, I noticed hair. "Gorgeous as ever, babe." I took in her smile, glad to see it before the inevitable seriousness of the situation hit everyone. That was my job, and I was a master. Lightening the moments, because fuck knows we needed it, especially the past year.

She immediately took in the atmosphere surrounding

us, though, perceptive as ever, and her face fell. "What's wrong?"

Cade came up behind her, pulling her back against him, and ducked down to speak into her ear. She bit her lip and nodded, her gaze darting to Zayde, then to me. "Do you want to speak to her on your own first?"

I guess I'd been designated as the official go-between for Jessa, not that I minded. "Yeah, I'll speak to her. Where is she?"

"Upstairs, I think. She went to lie down when we got back from the spa."

"I'll fill the others in," Cade told me, and I nodded, trusting him to get everything sorted. No doubt he had a plan in place already. While everyone headed into the lounge, I made my way upstairs. Jessa's door was open a crack, so I pushed it all the way open and entered.

My eyes went straight to the bed, and my mouth went dry. Jessa was lying on her stomach, reading, in a loose emerald green top and tiny shorts that clung to the curve of her ass, her legs kicked up and her dark hair spilling over her back.

My breath caught in my throat. *So fucking beautiful.*

Nothing had happened between us since the night at the club, and neither of us had expected it to since it was just one night of fucking, but my dick wanted her again. Now.

Stalking over to her, I pulled the Kindle from her hands, ignoring her startled squeak, and yanked her onto her back, throwing my body over the top of hers and bracketing her with my elbows on either side of her head. "Hi."

Eyes wide, she stared at me uncertainly, and instead of allowing her time to think, I lowered my mouth to hers.

Fuuuck. Kissing her was so addictive. She opened up to

me instantly, her arms winding around my neck, her legs shifting so I could slide between them. My tongue licked into her mouth, and my rapidly hardening cock ground against her softness. A tiny moan fell from her lips, and I kissed her harder before I realised that instead of kissing me back, she was now pushing me away.

"Wait." Her lips were shiny and swollen from our kisses, and I wanted to kiss her again. Okay, more than kiss. I wanted to fuck her so badly that I couldn't think straight. "No."

No.

I moved off her immediately, falling to the bed next to her, scrubbing my hand over my face. "Shit, sorry, Jessa. I didn't plan to do that."

She moved onto her side to face me. "It's nice to know you find me irresistible." There was a teasing smile on her lips, but her eyes were shuttered, and I couldn't read her. "I don't think we should..." Her voice trailed off, and she chewed at her lip. "It complicates things," she said eventually.

"Why? We both know where we stand. Nothing complicated about it."

A torn look came over her face, but then she shook her head, keeping her tone light and teasing. "No. Too much of a good thing, isn't that the saying? I wouldn't want to ruin you for your other women."

I still couldn't read her expression, so I went with it. I wasn't about to push if she wasn't into it, and even though my dick was protesting, I could easily call someone to take care of that when I was done here. My stomach churned with a weird feeling at that thought, for some reason, but I pushed it aside. Switching subjects to my original reason for being in her bedroom, I gave her a rundown of everything that had happened with Petr. "He wasn't there, but Cade and Z found your brother's phone number written down in his room."

"*What*?" She jerked upwards so hard that I almost rolled off the bed.

"Uh." I sat up, rubbing at the back of my head. "Yeah. We don't know why yet. We went to Creed's offices afterwards, but he's out of town until the weekend. We didn't want to say anything to your brother without speaking to you first."

"Thanks." Lying back down again, she blew out a heavy breath. "I don't know what to say. I don't know why he'd have my brother's number. I can't believe that Austin has anything to do with what's been going on. He's my brother. There has to be an explanation for this." Her voice was so sure, and I hoped like fuck that she was right.

"Yeah. Hopefully we can get some answers at the weekend. Cade doesn't think it's worth doing anything else until after that. Him and Z both agreed that it probably wasn't serious. All Littlefinger did was send that picture. He probably just wanted to scare you." I injected as much conviction into my tone as possible, even though I wasn't convinced.

She was silent, her brow creased in thought, her hands twisting in the bedsheets. Eventually she spoke, her voice quiet. "Maybe. I'd like some time alone now."

When I was closing the door, I heard her quiet "thanks" behind me.

Three-fifteen. Groaning, I rubbed at my eyes. What had woken me? Better not have been those bloody foxes again. I thumped my pillow, shifting onto my stomach.

A noise sounded from outside my room, and the sound sent fucking chills down my spine.

Not a scream, but a sound so terrified that I was up and out of bed before I knew what I was doing, bursting through the door of Jessa's bedroom and onto her bed. Pausing for a second, I tried to remember if you were supposed to wake people from nightmares or let them sleep, but then she thrashed on the bed, a pained whimper tearing from her throat, and that made my mind up for me. Shaking her shoulders, I dipped my head to her ear, urgently whispering her name. With a gasp, her eyes flew open, and she sat bolt upright in bed, shaking. She was illuminated by the dim glow of the bedside lamp that had already been on, and my gaze tracked over her, taking in her wild, panicked expression and sharp, shallow breaths.

"Jessa. It's okay. I'm here."

A choked cry escaped her, and she flung herself at me, burrowing against my chest. I didn't know what the fuck to do with myself, so I just held her, stroking her hair back from her face, whispering reassuring words that probably made no sense.

When she finally stopped shaking, she raised her head, twisting in my lap so she could meet my gaze. "I'm...I'm." A deep, shuddering breath made its way through her body. "Thank you."

I took in the way her bottom lip trembled and her wide, tear-stained gaze, still full of fear. Lifting my hand, I ran my thumbs gently across the dark circles under her eyes. "I'm not going anywhere."

She searched my face, and I didn't know what she was

looking for, but whatever it was, the fear disappeared from her eyes. "When I said no earlier..." Her quiet voice trailed off. Swallowing hard, she bit down on her lip, her lashes sweeping down, hiding her expression from me. "I want to forget my nightmares. I want to feel something...something good. Will you help me?"

This was such a bad idea. Fucking when she was in this vulnerable state? I opened my mouth, but then she leaned forwards and kissed me, her mouth hot and insistent against mine. As she straddled my thighs, my dick took over my brain, and I forgot all the reasons why we shouldn't do this. "Fuck," I groaned against her throat, sliding my hands under her pyjama top. We broke apart so I could pull it over her head, exposing her perfect tits, her nipples hard and begging to be sucked. "Is this what you want?" Cupping her ass and bringing her higher, I took one nipple into my mouth, flicking my tongue over the tip. A moan fell from her lips, the sound going straight to my erect cock. Fuck, I was so hard already, and I just needed to bury myself inside her.

"I need—"

"I know what you need, baby." I twisted her on top of me, her ass brushing against my bare cock, and I stifled a groan. When she was facing away from me, I eased her underwear down her hips, and then finally, she was completely bared to me. "So glad I sleep naked," I murmured, trailing kisses down her neck while I palmed her tits.

Her head dropped back against my shoulder, her fingers going down between her legs as she writhed against me, and the sight was so fucking hot that I had to force myself to think of the most unsexy things imaginable so I didn't come without even getting inside her. "You're so fucking sexy." My words were lost as I buried my face in her hair, sliding my hand down her stomach and between her legs to join her hand.

"Cass..." Her voice was so unsteady, so full of need, it made me want to bury my cock inside her and fuck her into the mattress until she was screaming my name. My cock jerked against her, and with effort, I kept my voice level, holding on to my control by a thin thread.

"My turn."

She obediently moved her hand out of the way, turning her head to capture my mouth in a messy kiss as I stroked over her clit, then eased two fingers into her tight, wet heat.

"Cass."

"Yeah, baby. Keep saying my name."

"*Cass*. Need you inside me. Now," she panted, gripping my hand and tugging. In an instant, she was spinning around on top of me, lifting up, and easing herself down onto my cock in slow, tortuous increments.

"You feel so good," I groaned when I was fully buried inside her. My hands gripped her ass as she rolled her hips on top of me. "Mmm. Just like that. Ride my dick."

Her lips touched mine. "Shut up and kiss me."

I could take a hint.

Our mouths met in a frenzied kiss. Holding her with one hand, I snaked the other between us, my fingers going to her clit.

"Oh, fuck." She tore her mouth away from mine, flinging her head back, her movements becoming erratic.

Thrusting up into her, I continued to work over her clit while she squeezed her pussy around my cock.

"I'm—ohhhhh." She shuddered around me, her rhythm completely gone as she lost herself in her climax.

So. Fucking. Beautiful.

My orgasm barrelled through me without warning, my dick pulsing inside her, filling her with my cum. I might have actually blacked out for a second, because the next thing I was aware of, my arms were around her while she rested her head against my shoulder, both of us breathing hard, our bodies slicked with sweat.

"You're literally gonna kill me one of these days," I mumbled into her hair. "I came so hard that I think I blacked out."

She huffed out a soft laugh, her arms sliding around me. Her lips pressed against my neck, then my jaw, and I smiled.

It didn't last for more than a few seconds before she was lifting herself up, her gaze shuttered. "I need to clean up."

The distance she'd suddenly put between us was more than physical. I wasn't sure why she was pulling away from me, but I wasn't going to leave her alone right now, in case the nightmares came back.

"I'm staying," I told her, and her eyes fluttered closed. She pinched her brow, already off the end of the bed and in front of the bathroom door. "Jessa. I'm staying," I said again, my tone allowing her no room for argument, and she sighed, opening her eyes and giving me a small nod.

I hid my own sigh of relief, turning away from her and climbing off her bed as the bathroom door shut softly behind her. While she was otherwise occupied, I used the opportunity to duck out of her room and into my own bathroom to clean up before I headed back into my bedroom. After pulling on a pair of boxers, because I had the feeling she'd be more comfortable with something between us, I left my room and made myself comfortable in her bed.

When she came out of the bathroom, her eyes darted to the bed, and she chewed on her lip while she stared at me.

"Come here." I patted the bed next to me. "You need to sleep."

She gave another one of those tiny nods and climbed in next to me, but lay right on the edge with her back to me, her body stiff and tense. I sighed and reached out, dragging her body against mine. "Sleep. *Just* sleep." Curling my arm around her waist, I dropped a kiss on her shoulder, then lay back on my pillow. Her body began to relax in small increments as I just held her, and eventually her breathing evened out and she slept.

I lay awake for a long time.

What was I doing here?

12

jessa

After that night where Cassius had seen me at my most vulnerable, seen everything I was trying to hide, I did my best to keep my distance from him. I'd warred with myself over staying with the Four or moving back to my apartment, but in the end, I knew I couldn't leave, not until I had answers about Petr. I'd had more nightmares, and Cassius had come in each time and held me until I fell asleep again, but I'd made it clear that I wanted nothing more than his comfort, and he'd respected that.

I was falling for him, and I knew that nothing would ever come of it. It wasn't easy to stay away, especially with his playful, flirtatious personality, the way he'd find opportunities to touch me, the way he made it clear he'd be down to fuck at any point. But I had to protect my heart. Things were fragile enough, and if I let myself continue down this path with him, it would hurt even more when I had to leave or inevitably see him with someone else.

He was so easy to love, though.

Tonight, he had on black trousers and a white shirt with

the top couple of buttons undone and his sleeves rolled up, showing his tattooed, golden skin, and the sight of him practically made my mouth water. I allowed myself one look at him before I tore my gaze away, focusing on the long bar in front of me, spirits of every kind lined up along the mirrored wall. We were back at Sanctuary again, this time to meet with Creed and to potentially confront my brother, depending on what Creed said. It was also Kinslee's birthday—Winter's best friend—so the mood was fairly upbeat, despite the worry of Petr hanging over us.

Lena slipped in next to me. "What are you drinking? I'll get these."

I turned to smile at her. "It's my brother's club. Drinks are on the house."

She grinned, scanning the shelves. "In that case, let's make the most of it."

Tequila it was.

Everyone partook of the shots, and my body relaxed as the alcohol fizzed through my bloodstream. I was aware of Cassius, but that was as far as it went. Tonight was about getting answers and celebrating Kinslee's birthday. Being Winter's best friend, she'd initially been wary of me being here. Winter must have explained something of my situation, though, because as soon as we'd all met up in the hotel lobby, she was nothing but genuine smiles.

Some of the group headed upstairs while Winter and Kinslee disappeared off to the loos, and Lena talked me into another shot, not that it took much persuading.

"Another?" she suggested when the tequila burn had faded from my throat, but I shook my head.

"Later. Let's pace ourselves." She nodded, and we made our way up to the VIP area, where my brother was going to be meeting us later in the evening. I followed Lena over to one of the huge booths, where the Four sprawled out along-side another guy. As we approached the booth, the guy stood, and I got my first good look at Credence Pope, aka Creed.

Intimidating was the first word that came to mind. The second was *wow*, because the man was absolutely gorgeous. Wrapped in a navy fitted suit, he studied me with eyes almost golden in colour, bright against his bronzed skin. His dark hair fell across his forehead, and the small scar on his left cheekbone and the air of danger surrounding him somehow added to his appeal.

"Creed. You must be Jessa." Even his voice was sexy. "Austin's sister, right?" A smile curved over his lips, and I shook myself out of my stupor. From the corner of my eye, I noticed Cassius' eyes narrow as he focused on us. What was all that about?

"Yes. Austin speaks highly of you."

He smiled again and took my hand, brushing a light kiss over the back of it. There was a soft noise behind me, and Creed's gaze flicked away, his smile widening. "Winter. Kinslee. This is a pleasure."

Spinning around, I watched with interest as after greeting Winter, he made a point of training his gaze on Kinslee, who wouldn't even look at him. "What's all that about?" I sidled up to Winter and spoke quietly in her ear.

She laughed. "Kinslee says he scares her, so I think he likes to take advantage of that fact. He's the same with Lena's friend, Raine, too. They both have this idea that he's dangerous."

"I guess I can see what they mean. Still, it seems like he enjoys it." The amusement dancing in Creed's eyes proved my point.

Winter smiled in agreement, then slid into the booth

next to Caiden, followed by Kinslee. Lena was already sitting on Weston's lap, and Zayde and Cassius were in conversation. As I hesitated at the end of the booth, the hostess appeared to take our drink orders.

Laura. The beautiful woman that Cassius had taken the number of last time we'd been here. His gaze darted to her, and he said something to Zayde, who slid out of the booth, letting him out. The second he trained that smile on Laura, his hand curling around her waist, I'd seen enough.

Fuck. Why did I have to develop feelings for him?

Biting my lip, I turned away. I felt a presence at my side, and I turned to look up into Creed's golden eyes. His gaze was inscrutable, but his eyes flicked between me and Cassius, and I'd bet anything that he'd read the situation correctly. His lips came down to my ear. "Show him what he's missing."

I jerked back, staring up at him. "Are you suggesting..."

"No. Not me." His lips kicked up at the corners. "Austin wouldn't appreciate it." A dark look flashed in his gaze. "And I have certain...tastes."

"I see." I didn't see. And I wasn't sure I wanted to see.

"But this club," he continued. "There's no shortage of willing participants, should you wish to show him what he's missing."

"He's not interested," I said in a low voice, glancing back to where Cassius was saying something that made Laura laugh, batting her lashes at him.

"Hmmm." Stepping back from me, he moved to Cassius and Laura, and I took a step closer, then another, keeping my gaze focused on the people on the main dance floor below.

"... mate ... anyone at the moment?"

I lost a few of Creed's words but heard enough to get

the gist of what he was asking Cassius. Cassius' reply was much louder. "Single as always." His wide, disarming grin as he glanced down at Laura was too much.

I'd heard enough.

Digging deep and gathering my composure, I flicked my hair from my shoulder, stood up straight, and turned on my heel, moving away from the booth and deeper into the VIP area. The whole section was dimly lit, and at the end, there was another bouncer standing in front of a black curtain. He straightened up as I approached.

Pausing, I turned to look behind me, seeing the back of Cassius' head as he leaned down to speak in Laura's ear. He hadn't even noticed I'd gone. And why should he? I meant nothing to him, and the sooner I got over this stupid crush, the better.

Turning back to the bouncer, I indicated to the curtain. "Can I go in there?"

He nodded. "You're free to go anywhere you wish, Miss De Witt." Okay, so he knew I was Austin's sister. His gaze scanned me in a purely professional way that had me relaxing. "Although, if I could offer a word of advice?"

I cocked my head, waiting for him to continue.

"Your brother might not enjoy seeing you in this part of the club. I'll give you a heads-up when he's on his way."

Now I was really intrigued. What was behind the curtain?

As soon as the bouncer drew it back and I slipped inside, I had my answer. Beyond a short corridor lay a room, all black on black, with glittering floors and mirrors along one wall, above a small stage with a pole. More booths were clustered around the space, each with a heavy curtain that could be closed around them. Some of the curtains were closed and some open, allowing me to see the bodies inside.

"Hi."

A tanned, muscular guy in the tightest shorts I'd ever seen bounded up to me.

"Uh. Hi?"

He grinned. "What's your poison? Man? Woman? Want to dance yourself? Whatever you want, we can provide it." He finished his speech with a flourish of his hands, his skin sparkling under the low lights.

"What is this room?" I returned his smile, more intrigued than ever.

"That, my darling, is a very good question." Reaching out, he grabbed my arm and tucked it through his, then led me further into the room. "This is where our VIP guests come if you want some more...personal entertainment." He indicated to the stage. "Dancers on the pole—the next one'll be on in half an hour or so. Then the booths—you can request a private dance if you so desire. We have a menu." A tablet suddenly appeared in his hand.

"Wait, where did that come from?" I glanced down at his ultra-tight silver shorts, confused.

"Wouldn't you like to know?" Tapping on the screen to wake it up, he showed me a list of dancers with colour codes next to their pictures, which he told me indicated who they would dance for and what dances they were willing to do. "It's all very safe. Classy, too. Despite the glitter."

"Oh. I had no idea this was here. Austin never mentioned anything—"

"You know Austin?" His eyes flew to mine.

"He's my brother."

Pursing his lips, he gave me an uncertain look. "Since you're his sister, and I'm his employee, I can't—"

"Please don't tell me that I need to leave. I can't go back out there."

"Why not?"

"Because the man I'm interested in is out there flirting with someone else, and he doesn't want me anyway, and I don't even want to want him," burst from my mouth in a rush.

"In that case...you need a distraction." The doubt disappeared from his eyes. Flashing me a grin, he swiped across the tablet screen. "I'll just book myself out..." His image on the screen darkened to show that he wasn't currently available. "I'm JJ, by the way. And I'm very, very gay. In case you were concerned about me getting handsy with you."

I laughed. "I'm Jessa."

He slid his hand into mine, leading me towards one of the open booths. "What would you say to a dance master-class from the master himself?"

The champagne flowed, and I lost track of time, grinding up against JJ, picking up the techniques he showed me. He proclaimed me a natural, and his praise warmed me through. This had been just what I needed.

Standing, he clasped my shoulders as one song ended, merging into the next. "I think you're ready to be set free."

"Set free?"

"Wait here." He headed over to the side of the room, and a few moments later, the lights changed from a sweeping pattern to a slow pulse, in time with the sultry beat of the music. Strutting back over to me, he flung himself into the booth. "Dance for me."

With a smile, I shook out my hair, threw him a wink, and began to move.

The music swept me away. I undulated my body over JJ's, spurred on by his words of encouragement and his wide grin. Spinning around, I arched back, sliding down his body, almost to the floor, before popping back up.

That was when I saw Cassius.

He stood way too close, his jaw tense and his blue eyes dark and stormy, laser focused on me and JJ.

For a second, I froze, before remembering his words about being single. Tearing my gaze away from his, I dropped my body back against JJ's, rolling my hips back.

"That's the guy you were trying to escape?" His head was close to mine, his voice soft, and there was no way Cassius would be able to hear him.

"Yes."

"He wants you."

I shook my head, moving my body on autopilot, even as I felt Cassius' gaze boring into me.

"Oh, he does." The next second, he slid out from behind me and was standing in front of Cassius. I came to a halt, my heart pounding as Cassius stared at JJ with a dark look I'd never seen on his face before, baring his teeth as he took in JJ's barely clad body.

JJ was completely unfazed, grabbing Cassius' arm and manhandling him into the booth. I almost smiled at Cassius' look of surprise as he found himself suddenly seated, but my heart was beating too fast, my mind whirling with confusion from the way he'd looked at me and JJ, and all I could do was stare at him.

JJ slid over to me, facing Cassius. He held a finger in the

air as he addressed him. "Rule. No touching the dancers. Otherwise, enjoy." Brushing my hair away from my ear, he leaned in, his voice dropping. "Dance for *you*, and make him work for it."

The music changed to a slow remix of "Such a Whore" by JVLA, and I closed my eyes, spun to face away from Cassius, and began to move.

When I spun back to face him, his eyes were even darker, and the same tense expression was on his face. Placing my hands on the smooth leather of the booth on either side of him, I rolled my body down his, and a harsh breath escaped him, his nostrils flaring as he clenched and unclenched his fists.

The realisation that he was trying to hold himself back from touching me brought a smile to my face, and I lifted my body up, straddling him but keeping myself raised so we weren't touching. I let my hair fall forwards and dragged my nails down his chest. He hissed through his teeth, his head falling back. The trousers he was wearing did nothing to hide the outline of his hard cock, and there was nothing I wanted more right then than to feel his hands on me.

"Jessa." A tortured groan fell from his lips, his gaze hot and dark, tracking all over my body.

"I don't know what the fuck's going on, but Austin's here."

The spell was suddenly broken at the new voice, and I jerked away from Cassius to see Caiden staring at us with something that looked a lot like disapproval.

"Here?" I couldn't disguise the panic in my voice, and that brought a smirk to Caiden's face.

"In the VIP bit."

My body sagged with relief. We were all adults here, but

I highly doubted my brother would want to see his sister grinding all over someone, especially not in this particular room.

Cassius shot out of the booth in the direction of the exit, and I followed him and Caiden, stopping to wave goodbye to JJ, who was balancing a tray of drinks on one hand as he headed towards one of the booths. He gave me a smile and a wink, and I smiled in return before picking up my pace to catch up with Caiden and Cassius.

I wished I hadn't. Their conversation was easy to hear.

"...you say that, but it didn't look like nothing."

Cassius made an irritated noise in his throat. "What do you want me to say? Yeah, so we fucked. Doesn't mean anything. We both know the score, so stop trying to make a big issue out of it."

I lost Caiden's reply as they disappeared through the curtain, but what I had heard was enough for me. It strengthened my resolve to get over him as soon as possible. I shouldn't have even danced like I just had, not for Cassius.

Straightening my short black dress, I paused to gather myself, and then I fixed a smile on my face and headed back into the VIP area with my head held high. It was time. Time to confront my brother, lay everything on the table, and get this Petr issue sorted once and for all so I could move back into my apartment and start picking up the pieces of my life. Alone.

13

cassius

Jessa's brother was deep in conversation with Zayde and Creed when I flung myself into the booth. Thank fuck for Cade—my dick was well and truly deflated after that near miss. I didn't want Austin's first impression of me to be a bad one. I studied him out of the corner of my eye as I reached for one of the beers that had magically appeared on the table. Both he and Jessa were hot as fuck, objectively speaking, and I could see a sibling resemblance, mostly in the dark hair and green eyes. Austin had a harder look to him, though, the look of someone more ruthless and cutthroat than Jessa was.

Introductions were made, and I managed to charm a smile out of Austin, leaving me leaning back against the booth, satisfied. Or I was until Jessa stormed up to the booth and slammed her hands down on the table.

Everyone stared at her in shock. She kept her gaze focused on Austin, not sparing the rest of us a glance. "Is there somewhere private we can talk?"

He exchanged glances with Creed before nodding. "Yeah, of course."

"Creed, too," she said. Then she glanced around the table. "Actually..." Hesitation entered her tone, and she chewed on her lip.

I wanted to kiss her.

What the fuck? Where did that thought come from?

"Everyone who was there that night, I guess." The way she emphasised "that night" needed no explanation.

It was decided that Lena would stay with Kinslee, since neither of them had been there that night, and Winter wanted to make sure Kinslee enjoyed her birthday. Some more of their uni friends were due to show up at any time, along with Raine, so they wouldn't be alone for long. We left them with a bucket of champagne and headed through a door into the back offices of the club, past the security room, and into a large, empty space with boxes stacked in one corner and a load of chairs piled on the other side.

"Storage," Austin said when he caught us glancing around the room. "Probably. Still getting our bearings here, the club hasn't been open long." He began arranging chairs in a kind of semicircle, so I went to help him, and soon we were all seated with Jessa the centre of attention.

"Okay. I'm just going to come out and say it because we need full transparency here." Jessa's voice didn't even waver for a second. This wasn't the Jessa I knew, who'd always followed in her dad's footsteps, never showing her hand unless she had no other choice. I guess she'd changed even more than I realised. She held her brother's gaze as she gave a rundown of the situation, somehow finding the strength to get through the whole story, never faltering once. I was so fucking proud of her in that moment.

Austin didn't outwardly react, casually reclined in his seat, and at first I thought it was because she'd downplayed the story, sticking to the basic facts, but when I took a closer look at him, I saw the hard set of his jaw and the way his knuckles were turning white as he gripped the armrests of his chair. He had one hell of a poker face.

Caiden and Winter both added to the story, filling in the gaps but also sticking to the facts, and when everyone was finally done, a heavy silence fell over the room.

The silence was eventually broken by Jessa. "Austin? Why did he have your number?"

Austin shook his head. "I honestly don't know."

"I might have an idea." Creed tapped his phone against the armrest of his seat. "From my intel, it seemed like he was acting alone... But...the Volkovs—"

"Who are the Volkovs?" Jessa asked the inevitable question.

"Russian Bratva. We're...negotiating quite an important vodka deal. Petr Ivanov was a known associate of the Stre-lichevos, who are...let's say...a Belarusian crime syndicate. In the simplest words possible, the Strelichevos are associates of the Volkovs, and we already knew that there was a connection between them all." His lips set in a flat line. "Having said that, we'd been assured that everything had been dealt with, but him showing up around this vodka deal—the timing seems suspect. It could be that Ivanov has managed to worm his way into the deal somehow."

Austin's expression turned thoughtful. "Could be. They wanted me to fly out to their distillery, but I've been too busy with the club opening, so our next step was going to be to set up a meeting with their contact, go through tasting options. If he's working with them, then maybe..." A darkness came into his eyes. "He's a marked man now."

As Creed gave him a brief nod, Jessa's shoulders slumped in relief, and I was unreasonably annoyed. I should be happy that they were here to save the day. But for some reason, I wanted the gratitude she was directing at them to be directed at me.

"We'll sort it. He won't get near you again, Jessa." Austin was out of his seat now, crouched down next to her and taking her hand in his. His gaze arrowed to Creed, who gave another short nod.

"If it turns out that he's working with the Volkovs, which is the only connection I can see, then we'll have to tread carefully. This deal we're negotiating is worth a lot of money for a lot of people." He pinched his brow. "The Volkovs are... You don't want to get on their bad side, trust me. But they have a code of honour. Although Ivanov hasn't directly disrespected them, by coming after you, he may have sealed his own fate."

Standing, he squeezed Jessa's shoulder. "Either way, consider it taken care of." She nodded, and he flashed her a smile that she returned with a small, genuine one that reached her eyes, and my stomach twisted with something that felt like jealousy but couldn't be. Maybe I had some kind of undiscovered hero complex.

What would my superhero outfit look like?

"Cass?"

I blinked, finding West waving his hand in front of my face.

"Sorry, mate. Must've zoned out for a minute there."

"Didn't realise we were that boring." He grinned as I stood, stretching. Zayde was off in the corner of the room, deep in conversation with Creed, and Jessa was talking quietly with Austin. As I watched, Austin straightened up, kissed the top of Jessa's head, then turned to me.

"Can I have a quick word?"

"With me?" My voice came out higher than normal, and he smirked.

"Yeah, you." Walking a short way from where Jessa was sitting, he waited until I was standing in front of him, then spoke again. "I just wanted to say thanks. She says you've been looking out for her." He ran his hand through his hair, suddenly looking frustrated. "I should've been there for her."

"You didn't know."

"Even so. I appreciate what you've done. If you ever need a favour, I owe you one." Stepping a little closer, he lowered his voice, discreetly sliding a business card into my hand. "Can you keep an eye on her? Even after she's gone back to her flat? I'm not asking you to spy on her or anything. Just...just let me know she's okay."

I licked my suddenly dry lips. "Yeah. I can do that."

"Good." With that settled, he spun away from me, raising his voice. "I don't know about anyone else, but I'm off the clock and I need a drink after all this."

"Yeah. I definitely need a drink." Jessa got to her feet, standing tall in her heels. She looked...lighter, if that made sense. Like a weight had been taken off. When she caught my eye, a smile curved over her lips, and she looked so fucking beautiful that all I could do was stand there frozen in place, staring at her.

West nudged me in the side. "Don't be so obvious. Her brother's watching you."

"What? Obvious about what?" I played it off, but he just raised a brow.

"I never thought I'd see the day," he muttered, but I didn't get a chance to ask what the fuck that comment was supposed to mean because the others were joining us.

Back in the club, Creed and Austin hung around, Austin bringing out some celebratory bottles of champagne for Kinslee that he swore was the best shit we'd ever taste, although to me it tasted like shit. I grimaced as the drink went down my throat, longingly eyeing the lone beer that remained next to the ice bucket.

Taking a quick glance in Austin's direction, I noticed his gaze sliding over to where Winter, Lena, and Kinslee were dancing with Raine and the other girls from Alstone College that had shown up. Specifically, to Kinslee. I couldn't blame him for looking—she was hot, although since Winter had moved in and Kinslee had been hanging out with us more, she'd become like a sister to me. While he was distracted by the view, I swapped out my champagne for the beer, ignoring the smirk Cade gave me.

Once the bottles of champagne were empty, Austin disappeared somewhere with Jessa, and the second I finished my beer, West was sliding over to me.

"I'm bored. Wanna check out the rest of this place?"

"Let's go." Following him out of the VIP area and down the stairs, I smiled to myself. When Weston and my sister had got together, I'd been worried that he wouldn't have time for me anymore. He was my best mate, and I was used to doing everything with him. I'd seen it happen before—couples getting lost in each other to the point where they forgot about their other friends. But my worries were unfounded. Anyone could see that he and Lena were loved-up, but both of them had their own shit going on, and my best mate had made sure that I didn't feel neglected.

We did a circuit of the main club floor, then ended up in the attached bar. It was packed, but we managed to grab a table and a couple of stools. West headed to the bar for drinks, and when he returned, he looked me dead in the eye.

"Jessa."

"What about her?"

"There's something going on between the two of you."

I sighed. I knew this conversation was coming. "There isn't, mate. We slept together, once—okay, twice—since she's been staying with us," I amended at his disbelieving look. "That's it, though. You know it doesn't mean anything. To either of us."

He sat back, making circles in the condensation on his glass. When he spoke again, his voice was quiet, his gaze fixated on the table in front of him. "You'd tell me if it was anything more than that, wouldn't you?"

"Course I would."

"Okay. I—" He broke off, shaking his head. "It's one thing to be helping her out, but after all the shit that's gone down, a relationship with her might complicate things. Her history with Winter, with Cade..."

"Huh? Who said anything about a relationship?" I stared at him. "How the fuck did you come to that conclusion? There's no feelings involved. It's just sex. Anyway, she isn't down to fuck anymore. She told me."

"Whether that's the case or not, you've been different with her."

"That's because I feel, I dunno, responsible for what happened. Whatever's gone down in the past, she doesn't deserve to be going through any of this shit, either. And she's trying, West. She's trying so fucking hard, and I can see that she's changed, and I'm sure you could, too, if you took the time to fucking notice." I was almost shouting by the end of my rant, and Weston stared at me, open-mouthed.

"Okay then," he said eventually. Picking up his pint, he downed it. "Another drink?"

Taking a deep, calming breath, I glanced at my own mostly untouched pint, then shrugged. "Yeah, alright." When he disappeared off to the bar, I gulped my beer, attempting to avoid thinking about the conversation that had just happened. Closing my eyes, I ran my hand down my face.

An image appeared in my mind, out of the blue and completely fucking unwelcome.

Jessa, grinding all over that stripper guy, both of them lost in their own world.

I gritted my teeth.

There were no feelings between me and Jessa.

None.

"Hey, did I show you this new drone I was thinking of getting?" West returned to the table, sliding a new pint to me. He tapped on his phone screen, and I'd never been more glad for a change of subject. After we'd had this drink, I was going to go back into the club, work my magic on a hot, willing, available woman, and prove to everyone that I didn't have a thing for Jessa.

Because I didn't.

14

jessa

Back at the Four's house the following afternoon, everyone was tired and hungover. I curled up on the sofa with my Kindle while Zayde and Caiden were setting up some new PS5 game. I was more comfortable here now, and it felt like I'd been accepted, however grudgingly, but I still had reservations. The biggest reservation being a certain blond god, who had spent the rest of the night in Sanctuary dancing with various women. I'd tried not to look, but...well, it was impossible not to. The only thing that made it bearable was that he hadn't taken any of them back to his hotel. Although, as I kept reminding myself on what felt like an hourly basis, I had no claim to him, and seeing him with someone else was inevitable.

But anyway, all this meant that I was on tenterhooks waiting for Austin to contact me so that I could finally move back into my flat. Time and space was what I needed most now.

"His turgid member throbbed as he thrust inside her quivering mound."

"Cassius!" My screech was probably loud enough to be

heard through the entire house. Cheeks flaming, I jumped up to snatch my Kindle back from him as he held it over my head. Somehow, he'd managed to sneak up behind the sofa and grab it from my hands before I could do anything about it.

Laughing uncontrollably, he held it out of reach. "Babe, I need to see what kind of questionable reading material you have here," he managed to choke out through his laughter. "Turgid member!"

"I seriously hate you," I muttered, giving up on the Kindle and collapsing back onto the sofa, burying my heated face in the cushions. Even Caiden and Zayde were laughing at me, or maybe at Cassius, who knew?

"No, no, wait. Listen to this." He cleared his throat dramatically. "Her moist channel sucked in his giant, pulsating rod, all the way to the root."

"Don't ever say the word 'moist' again." Now Winter had appeared, just to add to my embarrassment, and she accompanied her warning with a retching sound.

"Please, just stop," I begged, my voice muffled by the cushion.

"What the fuck are you actually reading?"

Raising my head, I glared up at Cassius, who grinned unapologetically at me. "It's supposed to be a fantasy story with elves and things. I didn't know there were scenes like that when I downloaded it."

"It's a fantasy, alright." A gleam came into his eyes. "Hey, let's go upstairs and re-enact the scene. You can see my giant turgid member up close and personal."

Out of the corner of my eye, I noticed Winter roll her eyes at Cassius as she swung herself into Caiden's lap, and I couldn't hold my laughter in any longer, despite my embarrassment. "That's such a flattering offer, Cass, but I'm going to have to say no."

The smile disappeared from his face, despite my teasing words. He handed my Kindle back to me, leaning down to my ear. "I bet if that stripper was here, you'd say yes."

What? My gaze flew to his. He was frowning, his lips pursed like he hadn't meant to say those words out loud.

"You mean JJ?"

Straightening up, he muttered, "Forget it," then made a point of going over to Zayde and asking about the game he was setting up. I stared after him, unsure of what to make of that comment that had come out of nowhere. One minute he'd been teasing me, the next—

There was no time to think about it any further when my phone started ringing, my brother's name flashing up on the screen.

I crossed my fingers for some good news.

A few days later, my bags were packed, and I was ready to move out. The last thing I'd heard from Austin was that Petr Ivanov was no longer a problem, and I didn't really want to know any of the details. It was enough to know that the threat was gone. Suffice to say, a weight had been well and truly lifted.

There was another bonus as well. Somehow, getting it all out in the open and having people actively wanting to help out had reduced my nightmares, too—I'd only had one since the club, and it was almost minor in comparison to the debilitating ones I'd been suffering with before.

Cassius, Weston, and Lena were the only ones to see me leave. After asking Lena to pass on my thanks and goodbyes to the others, I hugged her, and then Weston gave me an awkward half hug. I returned it, appreciative of him making the effort. He owed me nothing, after all.

My Mercedes had been driven back to my apartment building car park the previous week, because at the time we'd wanted Petr to think I was still there if he'd been watching my flat. Weston had been checking the surveillance feeds, but there hadn't been any sign of him, which we now knew was because he'd been in London, and now there was no need to continue checking the feeds because he'd been dealt with.

Anyway, all that meant Cassius was driving me home, and I couldn't help wondering if it was the last time we'd be alone together. Both of us had kept our distance since our interaction the day after Sanctuary, not that it had helped with the feelings I had for him. If anything, they were stronger than ever, but I made sure to never even give him a hint of them.

Cassius was uncharacteristically quiet on the drive back to my flat. I leaned against the window of his SUV, lost in my own head, and neither of us made any attempt to break the silence. When he pulled into the apartment car park, engine idling, I wasted no time in unsnapping my seat belt and getting out of there. Cassius was just as quick, jumping out of the car and opening the boot before I'd even reached it. When he pulled out my suitcase and placed it in front of my feet without a word, I got the hint. He couldn't wait to get rid of me.

I gripped the handle of my case and started around the side of the car. The lump in my throat grew.

I wouldn't cry.

"Goodbye," I managed, my voice barely a whisper, my words carried away by the morning breeze.

"Jessa. Wait."

The sudden urgency in his low tone brought me to a halt, level with the front grille of the SUV. I inhaled a shaky breath.

"Wait." His voice was much closer. Then he was there in front of me, cupping my face in his hands.

I stared up at him, unable to find any words to say.

"A goodbye kiss," he murmured, brushing his lips against mine. With a sigh, I gave in to the inevitable. He kissed me slowly, so slowly, like he was mapping out the contours of my mouth, sucking my bottom lip in between his lips before he slid his tongue into my mouth.

He held my face in place, angling me just the way he wanted me, pressing me against his car. My hands came up of their own accord, winding around his waist, pulling him closer. I could feel his growing hardness between us, but he didn't even attempt to do anything about it. Just kept on kissing me, long and slow and so fucking perfect.

Kissing me like I meant something to him.

The lump in my throat grew bigger, and I struggled to keep my composure.

When we finally broke apart, he just stared at me, looking shaken. His fingers came up to touch his swollen lips, his eyes wide and his pupils dilated.

"Bye," he said, his voice raw.

"Bye." Picking up my case, I moved around him in the direction of my apartment building.

This time, he didn't stop me.

I'd been back for an hour when the buzzer sounded to let me know that there was someone at the door. My heart stuttered before I remembered that the Petr threat was over, and I hit the button to answer the intercom. "Hello."

"Jessa. Let me in."

My heart stuttered for a whole different reason then. Pressing the key button to unlock the building's front door, I leaned my head against the cool wood of my own front door.

When the knock came, I swung the door open. Cassius stood there, shifting on his feet, tugging his bottom lip between his teeth, his brows pulled together.

"Want to come in?" Stepping back, I pushed the door as wide as it would go.

"I drove around," he said, taking a step into my apartment. "I drove. And I...fuck."

"Cass?" Moving around him, I clicked the door shut. He spun around, tracking my movements, and the frown disappeared, his gaze turning predatory.

My stomach flipped.

"I drove around," he repeated, "and then I came back."

My back was pressed against the wood of the door, and he crowded into my space. "Why did you come back?" There was no way I could disguise the breathiness of my voice.

"We had one last kiss." His body pressed against mine. "Now." His hands hit the wood on either side of my head. "We need." A press of his hips as he rolled them against me, and I sucked in a shaky breath. "One. Last. Fuck."

Then his mouth came down on mine.

He lifted me up, and my legs went around his waist, my back against the door, as we kissed and kissed and kissed, hot, rough, and messy, setting me on fire. I moaned into his mouth, and he pulled us away from the door, stumbling in the direction of my bedroom.

We didn't make it that far. Tearing his mouth away, he stared down at me as I attacked his neck and jaw with kisses, drawing out a growl of pleasure from him. "I can't fucking wait," he ground out, angling us to the left, and the next minute I was lying on a hard wooden surface while he tore the clothes from my body in rough, impatient movements. I barely registered that I was lying on my antique wooden dining table, rising up to rip his T-shirt over his head, then tugging down his jeans. No underwear, his cock sprung free, and I reached out, desperate to feel him.

"Not yet." His hands came to my shoulders, pushing me back down flat on the table. Then his arms were scooping up my legs, throwing them over his shoulders, and his hot mouth was on me, his tongue gliding across my wetness. My hands tugged at his hair as I shamelessly ground myself against his mouth while his tongue continued to drive me insane, the pressure so fucking perfect that I could already feel my orgasm building.

"Cassius. *Fuck*," I cried, arching off the table. My orgasm was sudden and blinding in its intensity, my body shaking against him as he kept up his intense movements, drawing out the pleasure to the point where I couldn't take it anymore.

When he raised his head with a wide, satisfied smile on his face, his lips glistening with the evidence of my arousal, I dropped my head back with a groan and closed my eyes.

There was no way I could look at him and hide the way I felt about him.

I was *so* fucked.

"I'm gonna come all over you."

My eyes flew open, and I forgot everything else as he stepped up to me, taking his erect cock in his hand and stroking himself over me. A few short strokes and his cum was hitting my body, his eyes never leaving mine.

"I...you..."

I gave up on words.

He curled his body over mine, and I reached up, running my hands across his strong back and up through his hair as he kissed me. Shifting, he moved so that he was lying on top of me, every inch of me covered by him.

There was an ominous creak.

Then a loud crack, and suddenly he was pulling us both backwards, falling to the floor with my body collapsed on top of his.

We exchanged glances, and I rolled off him, rising to my knees to look back at my dining table.

My now very broken dining table.

"Your table...was it from IKEA?" His voice turned up hopefully at the end.

I turned back to him, shaking my head. "Antique, actually."

He winced. "Maybe we can fix it."

A smile spread across my face, warmth unfurling in my chest as I took in how worried he seemed. "I never liked that table." Climbing to my feet, I held out my hand. "You said something about one last fuck, and I don't think that counted."

Heat flashed in his gaze. "Nope, definitely didn't count." He reached out lightning fast, swiping my legs out from under me and catching me as I fell, pulling me into his arms. Laying me down on my back, he stared down at me, brushing my hair back from my face. "But this one will."

I tugged him down to me, and he took the hint, covering my body with his. Raking my nails down his back,

I lifted my head to capture his mouth in a kiss. "Bring it on, Drummond."

A teasing smirk curved over his lips, but there was something about it that seemed forced. And the way he took me this time, slow, unhurried, worshipping my body... driving me close to the edge over and over before he finally let me fall...it felt different to the other times.

It felt like an ending.

15

cassius

"The summer's going way too fast." West flopped back on the grass, flinging his arm over his head. The football we'd been kicking around rolled to a stop at my feet, and I took the chance to drop onto the ground next to my best mate.

"Yeah." Staring out at the tree line, I had an idea. "Beach party?"

"When?" West tilted his head to glance over at me.

"Dunno. Friday?"

He nodded. "Sounds good to me. I'm surprised you haven't planned anything sooner than this, mate. I know how much you love any excuse for a party."

"Yeah...well...I haven't been in the mood for it. You know." I shrugged. That was changing, now. We were halfway through the summer break already, and before we knew it, we'd be back at uni for our final year—well, West had another year to go. Then we'd be out in the real world, working for a living, and long summer breaks like this would be a distant dream.

So, yeah. We needed to make the most of it. Right now.

"Invite as many single girls as possible. I wanna make the most of it." Flipping onto my stomach, I rested my head on my arms. "This is our last chance. Summer of fun, trademark."

"Did you just say 'trademark'? You can't trademark that sentence."

"I can."

"You can't."

"I can."

"You can't."

I sat up and grabbed the football and threw it at his head. That was the end of the conversation.

"Wanna play?" Caiden jogged over to us, followed by Zayde, and started showing off doing keepy-uppies with a smug grin on his face. He *knew* I was shit at them. Just had to rub it in, didn't he? I jumped to my feet and swiped the ball from him, running down to the small AstroTurf pitch we had in the garden. I laughed when I heard his shout, but he caught up with me within a few seconds.

"Fuck you," he said, grinning. "Two on two. Losers have to man the BBQ later."

Returning his grin, I nodded. "Me and Cade against West and Z," I called over my shoulder.

"What's wrong with you?" Winter stared at me over the top of her joint. We'd been relaxing on the deck after our BBQ, although the others had ended up in the hot tub, so Winter and I were the only ones remaining in the seating area.

"Me? Nothing. Why?" I raised a brow at her, reclining back on my chair. "Pass it over."

She handed me the blunt, and I took a long drag, my eyes falling shut.

"You don't seem as happy as normal." Curling her legs under her, she twisted to face me. "Anything you wanna talk about?"

"Nope."

After staring at me intently for way too long, she sat back with a sigh. "Spoken to Jessa lately?"

"Nope."

It was true. I hadn't, except for sending her a few texts checking in with her. I'd done a drive-by of her apartment block once or twice, and okay, I had West intermittently checking the feeds from the security cameras outside her apartment, but that was because her brother had asked me to keep an eye on her.

Maybe I also had a feeling...concern for her safety. Littlefinger had seemed almost too easy to get rid of, in my opinion.

Still, I didn't miss her or anything. She'd only been staying with us for a short time, and yeah, we'd slept together, but I had the feeling that Winter thought it meant more than it did.

You're in denial.

Shut the fuck up.

I shook my head with a growl, and Winter stared at me. "Everything okay?"

"Yeah, fine." Rubbing my hand over my face, I sighed. "Sorry, babe. Think I'm just tired."

She shuffled closer to me, resting her head on my shoulder. "I love you, you know that, right?"

"I know." Pressing a kiss to the top of her head, I slid my arm around her. "Wanna ditch Cade and get with me instead?"

"I heard that!" came from the hot tub, but there was no anger behind Caiden's words. Still, I threw up my middle finger just because, and Winter huffed out a laugh.

"Seriously, though, Cass." Tilting her head up, she met my eyes. "Don't hold yourself back because you think you need to act a certain way."

"What's that supposed to mean?"

"It means..." Pausing, she frowned. "I guess what I'm trying to say is, be open to new things. Possibilities. Maybe —" Cutting herself off, she bit her lip. "No. That's all I wanted to say. I want you to be happy."

"I am happy," I reassured her. "I'm always happy. Most of the time. You know nothing gets me down for long."

Taking another long drag of the blunt, she let the smoke curl through the air between us, then passed it over to me. "So, this party. Who's invited?"

A smile curved over my lips. "Everyone. It's gonna be a party to remember."

"I'd better come shopping for it with you, then. Someone needs to keep you in check."

"You're probably right."

"I always am."

The following morning, I somehow ended up in the computer room. It was Weston's domain, and now my sister had taken over part of it, too. Between them, they had a huge bank of monitors and a load of other computer shit. I didn't even know what half of it was for, and didn't really want to, but the important thing was that West had connected one of the computers to the security feeds around the Alstone College campus.

Including the university accommodation where Jessa lived.

Sliding into Weston's seat, I woke up the screen and input the password. The mouse cursor hovered over the internet browser icon for a few seconds before I gave in to the inevitable and moved it to the icon for the security feeds. I managed to get sidetracked from my mission by the first feed that popped up, watching a pair of seagulls fighting over what looked like half a hot dog, although it was hard to tell.

But once they'd flown away, I clicked into the feed of the camera facing Jessa's apartment building. There was no sign of her, not that I expected there to be, but I checked the feed for the car park, too, spotting her car parked in its usual place.

I stared at the feed for a while longer before I sat back with a frown. What was I actually doing here?

"Ready to go party shopping?"

With the best timing in the world, Winter stuck her head around the door, followed by Kinslee.

When we were in my SUV, Winter in the front and Kinslee in the back, I cranked up the music, throwing them both a grin. "Let's do this."

"Wait, Lena's—" Kinslee pointed towards the house, where the front door was wide open. Before I had a chance to respond, Lena came running down the driveway and threw herself into the back next to Kinslee.

"Can you drop me at Raine's house on the way?"

"Do I look like your personal taxi service?" I shook my head, meeting her gaze in the rear-view mirror.

"Yep." She gave me a wide smile, and I sighed loudly.

"I suppose I can go out of my way just this once."

I'd been driving for about ten minutes when I realised

we were going in the wrong direction. And when a certain Georgian apartment building came into view and my foot automatically eased off the accelerator, slowing us down to a crawl, I groaned under my breath.

Maybe no one had noticed.

"Ahem." My sister gave a loud, fake cough from behind me, and I glared at her in the mirror. Next to her, Kinslee raised a knowing brow, smirking, and I could feel the weight of Winter's stare boring into the side of my head.

"Stop it, all three of you." I spun the wheel, speeding up as I manoeuvred us back onto the main road.

"We didn't say anything." Winter's voice was far too innocent, and I scratched the side of my face with my middle finger, right where she could see it, which just caused them all to start laughing.

"Cassius and Jessa, sitting in a tree—"

"I will throw you out of my fucking car," I growled at Lena. Meeting Kinslee's amused gaze, I gave her a hard look. "Don't even think about saying anything."

She clamped her mouth shut, but her eyes were still dancing with amusement. Despite myself, I found a smile appearing on my lips.

I could handle a bit of harassment from the three of them. When the party came and they saw that I was my usual self, taking my pick of hot, willing women, they'd forget all about teasing me about Jessa.

Everyone would.

16

cassius

"I don't think that was enough." Stepping back, I studied the bonfire I'd built on the beach with the help of Cade and Z. "Let's chuck some more on."

Zayde sloshed another load of lighter fluid on the logs, and the three of us watched in satisfaction as the flames shot into the air.

"Speaking of fire, that reminds me." Cade stepped closer, lowering his voice and running a hand through his dark hair, a frown on his face. "What's that boarding school your—is it your cousin?—goes to? Went to? That really strict one?"

"Yeah. Uh. I can't remember the name. I can ask my dad, though. Why?"

He sighed. "Roman. My fucking idiot of a cousin. You know he got suspended from his school for arson? Well, now he's got himself expelled, something to do with flooding the basement classrooms, I think. Not sure. Even my dad couldn't get him reinstated, so I said I'd ask you about your cousin's one. They're not allowed phones or anything, are they?"

"So the rumours go." I tried to remember what I'd heard of it. "Don't think they're allowed any contact with anyone outside the school during term time."

A smirk appeared on his face. "That'll go down well with Roman."

"I'll get the info from my dad and pass it on."

"Cheers, mate." He flashed me a quick grin before turning back to stare at the fire. "Want a beer?"

When he was off getting the drinks, I threw myself down on the sand next to Z. "I never thanked you."

"For what?" He turned to stare at me, surprised.

"The whole Creed thing. Y'know. If you weren't connected to him, things might not have worked out so well for Jessa. For any of us, in fact, if we include all the shit that went down in the past."

"You're thanking me for knowing someone?" One brow raised, just a tiny bit, and I rolled my eyes.

"You know what I mean. I don't think you give yourself enough credit."

"Maybe." His voice was noncommittal. I sighed. I'd known the guy for years, and sometimes he was just as hard to read as the first day we'd met. Zayde was an impenetrable vault, unless he wanted to let you in. Even then, he only let you see bits and pieces of him.

Tearing my mind away from the mystery that was Zayde Lowry, I changed the subject. "Did your dad give you the MBA talk?"

He stared at me blankly. "No. What?"

"Oh. My dad said that they're hoping to get us straight into working at Alstone Holdings once our final year at uni is done, but they're gonna be offering us all the opportunity to do an MBA part-time while we work. You know, add more strings to our bows or whatever the saying is."

He turned to stare into the flames. "Once my degree's finished, I'm done with learning."

"Fair enough."

We lapsed into silence, both watching the flickering flames, but it was comfortable, knowing that I didn't have to make conversation, that Z was happy enough to just chill without me needing to fill the silence. It was one of my favourite things about him, if I thought about it.

Caiden returned with his arms full of beers and dropped to the sand next to Z. "Here. I got us two each. Saves us having to make an extra trip."

"Good thing I got my own. "

I twisted my head to see West standing behind us. Grinning, I thumped the sand next to me in an invitation, and he took it. When he was seated, I uncapped the bottle Cade handed me. "To us. For being the four amazing fuckers that we are."

There were snorts of amusement, which I ignored, but everyone joined me, clinking bottles together with a "cheers."

I fucking loved my friends.

Around an hour later, when I found myself scanning the crowded beach for the fiftieth time, I'd had enough. This wasn't me. I headed over to one of the coolers, swiping another beer, then made my way over to a group of four girls from one of my classes, noting their admiring smiles as I strolled over. After placing my beer on the crate they were balancing their drinks on, I threw my arms around the shoulders of two of the girls. "Ladies. You're all looking beautiful tonight."

Gem, the girl on my left, angled her body into mine, batting her long lashes as she stared up at me. "We've missed you since uni finished."

"Yeah. We haven't seen you around for ages." Su pouted, stepping closer and placing a proprietary hand on my chest. As the four of them crowded around me, I started to panic. Something was wrong.

Really fucking wrong.

Four fit as fuck girls were right here, any of whom would probably sleep with me, given the chance. I'd slept with three of the four already, and from the way they were running their hands over me and giving me those looks, it was a sure thing that they'd be interested in a repeat.

But my dick wasn't even showing any interest.

Studying the curves of Gem's tits, I experimentally slid my hand down onto her ass, and she gave me a sultry smile.

Nothing.

Not even a twitch.

My worst nightmare had come true.

My. Dick. Was. Broken.

I was pulled out of my spiralling panic by Su tapping my arm with her manicured nails. From the raised brow she was giving me, it wasn't the first time she'd tried to get my attention.

"Sorry, babe, what was that?" I flashed her an apologetic grin.

"I said, I'm surprised she's here. Did you know she was coming?"

I followed the line of the other girls' gazes, looking over the top of their heads.

Jessa.

Her gorgeous body was wrapped in a red bikini, her

dark hair blowing in the early evening breeze, and she looked so beautiful that I was temporarily stunned.

No. It wasn't her beauty that was stunning me.

It was the realisation that flooded through me the second I saw her. Two realisations, in fact.

One, my dick most definitely wasn't broken. Not anymore. And two—which directly related to the first point —when it came to Jessa De Witt?

I was completely and utterly fucked.

She stood on the fringes of the group, chewing on her lip the way I knew she did when she was nervous, and I willed her to find her strength. She'd come far from the hollow shell of herself that she'd been for so long, but I guess this was her first test, being surrounded by so many people that she knew, people that had witnessed her fall from grace and the way she'd hidden herself away from everyone.

Her gaze darted around, wide and worried, and I took a step forwards, to do what, I didn't know. But then, her eyes met mine.

"I invited her," I murmured in reply to Su, holding Jessa's gaze. A small, hesitant smile curved over her lips, and then I took another step forwards, slipping my arm from around Gem and beckoning her to me.

My own smile widened as she straightened her shoulders, tossed her hair, and strutted across the sand towards me, acting like the queen she was deep inside. When she was close enough to touch, I lunged forwards, sweeping her up into my arms.

She threw her arms around my neck, laughing.

My stomach flipped, and there was an unexplainable ache in my chest that hadn't been there before.

"What a welcome." Her voice was breathless as she stared up at me through her lashes.

I swallowed hard. "I missed you." My words came out low and rough, dragged from my lips without any conscious thought.

Fuck.

She searched my face, probably reading my spiralling panic far too easily. Instead of replying, she tugged my head down, her soft lips moving over mine.

I kissed her back, my tongue stroking into her mouth, pulling her even closer so the curves of her body were pressed against mine, and even that wasn't enough.

I wanted more of her. To consume her.

Like I said.

Completely and utterly fucked.

17

jessa

My heart was pounding, both with the adrenaline of just being here at the party—arriving on my own and garnering everyone's attention in the process—and the effect that Cassius had on me.

He said he missed me.

I tried not to read anything into his words, especially since he looked like he regretted saying them the second they were out of his mouth. Pulling back from him with a smile and gently disentangling my body from his, I kept my words light. "I could definitely get used to that kind of welcome. Now, I need a drink and a dance, in that order. I'll see you later?"

He didn't say anything, and I figured he might need some time to himself, so I left him to it, ignoring the pointed glares from the girls he'd been standing with—presumably because I'd kissed him. The old me might've made a bitchy comment, but I had no desire whatsoever to intentionally upset anyone now, so I pretended like I didn't notice them and headed in the direction of the nearest coolers.

"Jessa!"

Spinning around, I saw Winter waving at me from where she was dancing close to the fire with Kinslee and a group of girls from Alstone College. I grabbed a drink and made my way over to them, returning their greetings and taking slow sips from my can of premixed cocktail. There was no hostility from any of them, and I relaxed, moving my body to the music almost on instinct, my mind drifting as the sounds of the party filled the air around me.

Kinslee and a couple of the other girls disappeared, making the trek up to the loos at the top of the cliff. When they'd left, Winter sidled over to me, lowering her voice. "He hasn't stopped watching you."

"Who?"

"You know who." She stared at me for a minute, then seemed to come to a decision. "I'm not interfering, but I just want to say...Cass is one of my best friends, and I love him. I—"

"I'm not going to hurt him, Winter. Not if I can help it."

Shaking her head, she frowned. "No, that wasn't what I was going to say. I was going to say that he's sensitive. He hides a lot of it behind his jokes, but he's... I just think he could get hurt easily, you know?" Placing her hand on my arm, she squeezed lightly before stepping back. "Please don't take it the wrong way. It's not you hurting him that I'm worried about. It's... Look, can I be honest?"

"Please do." I glanced around us. "Do you want to talk about this somewhere a bit more private?"

"Yeah."

We headed around the other side of the fire and sat on

one of the blankets that had been laid out, and then Winter picked up the thread of our conversation.

"Okay. I'm worried that he might not open himself up to anything with you until it's too late, and by too late, I mean that he might fuck things up between you before he decides he wants anything more. And you might not want anything to do with him by the time he's worked out what he wants—which you'd be well within your rights to do—but I have the feeling that by then he'd be in a lot deeper than he realised." A frustrated huff escaped her. "I'm not explaining this properly."

Moving into a cross-legged position, I leaned back on my hands. "I think I get what you're saying. I know he has a sensitive side—he's got a huge heart, and I know how much he cares for the people that are close to him. But I really don't think that you need to be worrying about this. Cassius likes variety way too much to want to settle, not now at least, and especially not with me. Fuck, Winter. I'd be just about the worst choice for him. I'm not exactly relationship material, and the way I've acted in the past, especially to you...who wants a constant reminder of that?"

"Stop that right now." Her voice was fierce, and her blue eyes flashed with anger as she looked at me. "Stop putting yourself down. I already told you I forgive you, and I know the others are over it by now. Life's too short to hold petty grudges."

"But." Tears filled my eyes, and I struggled to speak over the lump in my throat. The words slipped out, raw and broken. "Sometimes I look at myself in the mirror, and I *hate* myself. I don't know how to get over that. I don't know how to be me anymore."

"You do." Winter moved closer and slid her arm around me. I was so surprised that I froze before I forced my body to relax again. "You *do* know how to be you. You've been doing it for months now. You went through a fucking awful experience that got dragged up again, and yet you've come through it. You're beating your nightmares—"

"How did you know about them?" I asked in a whisper.

She leaned her head on my shoulder, her hair soft against my skin. "I heard you, and I've seen Cass going into your room. None of the others know, I don't think. I have them, too, sometimes. Nightmares about Caiden being shot." Her voice wobbled. "I-I thought he was dead. I love him more than anything in this entire world, and I thought I'd lost him."

"I'm so sorry." I straightened up so I wasn't resting on my arms and hugged her to me. "I can't even imagine what you went through."

"Yeah. It fucking sucked." She sniffed, raising her head and running her thumb under her eyes. A sad smile twisted her lips. "Even now, it still hits me, normally when I least expect it."

We were silent for a while, lost in our own memories.

Finally, she spoke again. "My point is that the good days eventually start to outweigh the bad, and you get through it, and I can see you're getting through it. You've changed, a lot. You look like the old you again on the outside, but on the inside, you're different. Softer. Nicer." She gave me a small smile. "I think anyone would see that if they took the time to look. And Cass...he's taken the time to look. I just hope that he doesn't take too long to realise what he has right in front of him."

"I like him. *Really* like him. I tried so hard not to, but it was impossible."

"The allure of Cassius Drummond."

"Yeah." I sighed. "I'm basically fucked."

She laughed softly, dragging her thumb under her eyes again. "Ugh. This whole conversation was a lot more emotional than I'd planned on."

"It was, but I'm glad we had it." Returning her smile with a tremulous one of my own, I indicated my head towards the other side of the fire where the girls were dancing. "Drink and dance?"

"Yep."

"Can we talk?" A low voice murmured in my ear, and a tanned, tattooed arm snaked around my waist. Leaning back against Cassius' firm torso, I craned my head around to look at him, unable to stop my smile.

"Yeah, of course."

"Not here." Releasing me, he spun me around to face him. The seriousness in his gaze made my smile drop.

Threading his fingers through mine, he led me down to the water's edge, close to the rocks over at the far side of the beach. The waves lapped against the shore where we stopped, and I stepped out of my flip-flops, picking them up with my free hand and digging my toes into the wet sand.

"You broke my dick." He accompanied his statement with a huge sigh, his shoulders slumping.

"Excuse me?" Releasing his hand, I placed my flip-flops behind me on one of the rocks, away from the waves, then turned back to him, placing my hands on my hips.

"You heard me."

I couldn't help smiling at his face. Yeah, he really wasn't happy with...actually, I wasn't exactly sure what he was talking about, but I was sure I could coax him into telling me. Moving so I was in front of him, I took a chance and ran my hands up his arms and then back down again, noting the shiver that he instantly tried to suppress. "Can you explain what you mean?" I rolled my hips against his, a light, teasing touch. "Because it doesn't feel very broken to me."

He groaned, rubbing his hand over his face. When he finally lowered it, he looked down at me, his gaze almost tormented. "Four girls. All hot. I could've had any of them, but my dick..." Trailing off, he glared down at the hardening bulge in his board shorts as if it had personally offended him.

"And that's my fault, how?" I trailed my hands back up his arms and hooked them around his neck. Tilting my head, I placed an open-mouthed kiss to the underside of his jaw. "Because you're hard for me and not for them?"

"*Yes*," he growled, gripping a handful of my hair and tugging my head back, his mouth going to my throat.

When he raised his head with satisfaction in his gaze, I knew I'd have a mark where his mouth had been. "Feel better now?" I asked.

He shook his head with a frown, and I pressed another kiss to his jaw. My hips moved against his in the barest increments, just enough to tease us both but not enough that it would draw the attention of any of the others around. His hand tugged on my hair again, but this time, his lips met mine, his kiss fierce and intense.

Fuck. Being kissed by Cassius Drummond...nothing and no one compared to him. Nothing even came close.

"Are you sure it's my fault?" My fingers stroked through his hair, my nails lightly scraping across his scalp. "I don't control your cock."

"You do," he muttered, his lips tracking across my skin from my mouth to my ear, where he stopped.

Barely discernible, his next words, breathed rather than spoken, had my heart stuttering to a halt.

"Do you want to be exclusive fuck buddies?"

My heart roared back to life.

"*What?*" I pulled back from him so suddenly that I stumbled, and I had to dig my feet further into the sand to regain my balance. He watched me with a look that I really couldn't read.

"I'm serious."

He was? I didn't know what to do with myself. My legs had gone all shaky, and I needed to sit down. This was something I hadn't been prepared for in any way, especially not after my conversation with Winter and my constant reminders to myself that I'd be seeing him with other women sooner or later. I stepped over to the rocks and collapsed down onto one.

Cassius crouched down in front of me, placing his hands on either side of my legs. "I'm serious," he repeated. "Think about it."

Did I want this? Being exclusive with Cassius was both the best and worst thing I could imagine. Best, because I'd have him, even if only in one way, and worst, because when the arrangement ended, my heart would be the one that was shattered.

Winter's earlier words came to my mind. *Cass...he's taken the time to look. I just hope that he doesn't take too long to realise what he has right in front of him.*

Maybe this wasn't quite what she was thinking of, but here he was, asking me to be exclusive, even if the reasons were strictly dick-related.

And then I looked at him. Really looked at this amazing

man, with the biggest fucking heart of anyone I knew, who was here right in front of me waiting patiently for my answer. Choosing *me* over any other girl.

My decision was easy. Even if I only got to have him for a little while; even if it left me broken, it would be worth it.

So worth it.

"Okay."

"Okay?" His lips curved upwards, and I nodded, my own smile tugging at my lips as I took in the happiness on his face.

"Yeah. So how does this work, anyway? I've never had an exclusive arrangement before."

Rising to his feet, he took my hands and pulled me up, then slid his arms around my waist. His eyes darkened as he stared down at me. "Me neither. I'm thinking it'll involve a lot of my dick being inside you." He nipped at my bottom lip. "Whenever and wherever we want."

"Oh, really?" I arched a brow. "I guess I can agree to those terms."

"Good." I felt his smile against my lips before he kissed me.

When he pulled back again, I met his gaze. "Exclusive. So no sex with anyone else?"

"That's what exclusive means."

"No kissing anyone else?"

"No." His voice was hard. "No kissing. No touching. I don't want you even looking at anyone else."

"Wow, Cass. I didn't realise you were so possessive. This goes way beyond the realm of fuck buddies."

A muscle ticked in his jaw as he glared over my head at nothing in particular. "So? We can make our own rules."

"Okay. I can do that. I want to do that." I ran my hand up his back, placing a kiss to his lips, and his expression softened. Curling my other hand around his neck, I used my thumb to stroke across his skin. "I won't hold you to that, though. The kissing, and the touching, yeah, if we're going to be exclusive, but I don't expect you to not even look at anyone else."

He kissed me so softly that it made me melt inside. When he drew back, his eyes met mine, the blue even brighter than normal, the reflection of the setting sun making them shine with golden tones.

I'd been lying through my teeth. If he even looked at anyone else...

This was *so* bad. I had to protect my heart.

That look in his eyes, though...it broke through every single one of my defences. And when he spoke again, I knew I was already hopelessly lost.

"I only want to look at you."

18

jessa

After the party had ended, Cassius had come back to my apartment, and we'd spent the night getting reacquainted with each other. He'd stayed over but had left early in the morning to do some family thing with Lena and their parents. Building on my conversation with Winter, I'd decided not to mope around inside all day, so I'd spent an hour talking with my brother before I'd arranged to meet one of my classmates for coffee in town for the first time since the incident at the docks.

While I was out, the texts had come through, but I hadn't read them until I'd returned home, by which point I had six waiting for me—although four of the six were just GIFs.

Sex God: Busy tomorrow?
Sex God: *inquiring minds want to know GIF*
Sex God: Jessaaaaaaaaaaaa

Then, about an hour later, there were three in quick succession:

Sex God: *tapping watch GIF* *waiting GIF* *bored GIF*

Smiling to myself, I replied.

Me: I assume you're the one who changed your contact name in my phone to sex god
Sex God: YOU'RE ALIVE *shocked emoji*
Me: Always so dramatic Cass
Sex God: Did I dick you so good that you passed out and couldn't answer for FOUR HOURS?
Me: Yes that's exactly what happened *eye roll emoji* *laughing emoji*
Sex God: Thought so. So???
Me: I'm free. Want to come here or should I come to you?
Sex God: Neither. Wanna see me beat you at crazy golf?
Me: Like a date?!
Sex God: No like a starter before the main event
Me: The main event being???
Sex God: Don't pretend you don't know. You're dying to ride my dick again
Me: Am I?
Sex God: Yep. Pack a bag and prepare to be sore tomorrow
Me: Big promises
Sex God: Big dick
Me: BIG ego
Sex God: With good reason
Me: OK I feel like this could go on for a while. To answer your question, yes I'd love to beat you at crazy golf

Me: And the rest. Thanks for inviting me x

Sex God: You mean you'd love me to beat you. If I win do I get a treat? My cock in dsgfkk

What was that supposed to mean? I stared at my screen, frowning, then another message came through.

Sex God: This textual foreplay is disgusting *puke emoji*

I was even more confused by this point, until I received the next response.

Sex God: Sorry my ANNOYING AS FUCK SISTER stole my phone. I'll pick you up at ten

Even though the thought of Lena reading some of those messages made me grimace, I couldn't help laughing at the way they acted towards each other. How much had she read? Not that there was particularly anything to hide, but there were some things that you really didn't want your siblings to see.

As if he read my mind, he replied a couple of seconds later.

Sex God: She only saw the last few messages

Sex God: See you tomorrow

Me: OK

I hesitated for a minute, then added a heart at the end of the message, instantly regretting it in case he thought I was pushing for more. But a few minutes later, my phone lit up with another text.

Sex God: *heart emoji*

Standing in my apartment window, I scanned the street. My spine prickled with awareness, and an uneasy feeling rolled through me. There was a flash of movement below, and I jumped before realising that it was just a cat.

I guess it would take a while for me to stop seeing things in the shadows.

The unease was wiped away when a matte black SUV pulled up to the kerb, and I quickly grabbed my small overnight bag and made my way downstairs.

This isn't a date, I reminded myself. Still, when I stepped outside of my apartment doors to see Cassius grinning at me, his arm casually leaning on the window of his SUV and sunglasses covering his eyes, my heart skipped a beat.

"Hi."

"Hi." A small, shy smile pulled at my lips. I rounded the car and climbed in, throwing my bag into the back.

Cassius started up the engine, glancing in the rear-view mirror, his hand resting on the steering wheel.

He paused, his gaze flicking across to me. I didn't even get a chance to take a breath before he was leaning across the centre console and slanting his lips over mine.

The kiss was over as quickly as it had begun, but it was enough to send butterflies racing through me. And when Cassius manoeuvred away from the kerb, the smile on his face was different to his usual cocky grin.

Notadatenotadatenotadate, I repeated in my head, enough times that it eventually sunk in by the time we reached the crazy golf course. We picked up our clubs and golf balls—yellow for me, green for Cass—and made our way onto the pirate-themed course. It was set partway up a cliff, overlooking the sea and the pier, and was unsurprisingly busy since it was the middle of summer.

What I couldn't work out was why Cassius had invited me on what would have been a date to anyone else, or I guess a friendly thing *if* we hadn't been sleeping together. But whatever was going on inside his head, I was happy. Happy to be here, spending time with the man I was falling for, just me and him.

"How did Lena manage to steal your phone yesterday?" I asked as we attempted to hit our golf balls up a miniature gangplank.

Cassius huffed. "She came out of nowhere like a bloody ninja, right when I was in the middle of replying to you. She owes me, big time. Even more than before."

Twirling my club around, I eyed my ball's destination before stepping up. A quick tap, and it rolled the short distance up the gangplank, coming to a stop at the top next to Cassius' ball. "What did she owe you for before?"

"I voluntarily sexiled myself for the night when she moved into our house at the start of the summer, okay, mostly so I didn't have to bleach my eyeballs and ears. But she owes me for that, and now she owes me for this, too." He pulled a face as he hit his ball far too hard, sending it flying through the open jaws of a shark and straight past the hole, rebounding off the wooden board.

"That's terrible."

"I can sense your sarcasm, you know." His hand shot out, and he grabbed me around the waist, his fingers tickling my sides. I let out a loud shriek, scrambling away from him.

"Babe, come back here. I just wanna cuddle." Holding

out his arms, he gave me an innocent, wide-eyed look, but I wasn't fooled.

"Fuck off."

A hard glare came from a woman at the hole next to ours, accompanied by about five kids. She stepped up to me, shoving her finger at my chest. "Mind your language! There are children present!"

"Sorry." I pulled a contrite face, ignoring Cassius practically collapsing with laughter.

"Disgusting behaviour. In public, as well!" Her outraged mutters continued as she turned her back on us and marched back to her own hole.

"Oh, Jessa." Cassius had recovered from his laughing fit, and he came up behind me, leaning down to speak in my ear, all low and husky. "What a dirty, dirty mouth you have."

I shivered at his words.

Then he had to ruin it.

"You should wash that dirty mouth out. With my c—"

Reaching up, I slapped my hand over his mouth. "Don't you dare finish that sentence. There are children present, remember."

He laughed against my hand, and after a second, I joined him.

We made it around the rest of the course without incident, Cassius proclaiming himself the King of the Pirates when he received a pirate hat made of cardboard as his reward for winning the game. He wore it for all of five minutes, took about a hundred selfies for his social media, then decided he'd had enough of wearing it.

After stowing the hat in the car, he turned to me. "I'm hungry. Want to get some food?"

I stared up at him, surprised. I'd assumed that we'd go

back to his place after golf, but if he wanted to spend more time out here with me, I'd take it. "Yeah, okay."

He gave me a blinding grin. "Good."

The not-date-date continued with chips down at the seafront. When we'd finished the last of them, he threw our bags in the bin and came jogging back over to me. I watched the people around us admire him, and I was once again struck with disbelief that he'd chosen to spend time with me, out of everyone.

"Ice cream?" His hand reached out, and his fingers brushed against mine as I nodded. When we stepped up to the ice cream kiosk, he wrapped his arms around me from behind, resting his chin on my shoulder, and it took everything in me to concentrate on the ice cream flavours listed rather than the feel of his body against mine.

"Uh. Strawberry with clotted cream, please," I told the white-haired woman at the kiosk after Cassius had placed his order. "I've got these." Pulling my debit card from the pocket of my shorts, I handed it over.

"I was gonna get those," he complained, placing a soft kiss to my cheek.

"Too late."

He kissed me again.

"Young love." The woman sighed dreamily from behind the counter, and I felt Cass smile against the side of my face. The fact that he made no move to correct her shouldn't and didn't mean anything, but my heart still sped up at the thought of us being a real couple. It was all too easy to imagine right then.

When we both had our ice creams, I turned to head down onto the beach, and Cassius fell into step next to me. His free hand brushed against mine again, but this time, he threaded his fingers through mine.

The butterflies inside me were going crazy.

Not a date, remember.

To distract myself, I took the first taste of my ice cream, swiping my tongue over the melting strawberry creaminess.

"Ohhhh," I moaned as the delicious taste burst on my tongue. "This is *so* good." I licked around the sides, catching the drips before they made their way down the cone. "How's yours?"

When Cassius didn't reply, I turned my head to see him staring at my mouth, his own ice cream dripping over his hand unnoticed.

"Cass?"

"I can't do this," he muttered to himself. He tugged at my hand, turning us in the opposite direction from where I'd been heading, leading me under the pier. It was quiet under here, most people preferring to bask in the sun.

"Can't do what?" I asked him when he came to a stop next to one of the huge wooden supports that held up the pier.

"Do you have any idea how fucking difficult it is to not get a boner around you?"

Oh. I smiled. "Sorry?"

"You're not sorry." He crowded up against me so my back was to the wood and leaned down. "Licking that ice cream like that and moaning. My dick is big, babe. That means I can't hide my boner in public, not in these shorts." His tongue darted out, and he swiped some of my ice cream as he pressed into me.

"I wouldn't rub up against me if you want it to go down."

"How are you so unaffected?" He stared down at me, his pupils dilated.

Angling my head forwards, I tasted his ice cream. Chocolatey deliciousness, rich and smooth, slid across my tongue. "Mmm. So good. I—"

His mouth came down on top of mine before I had a chance to finish the rest of the sentence. When we broke apart, both of us were breathing heavily, and our ice creams were dripping everywhere.

"I'm not unaffected," I said breathlessly. Taking hold of his free hand, I placed it over my left breast. "Feel my heart rate. Feel how hard my nipples are."

He ran his thumb over my nipple, circling it, and I moaned softly.

"If you moved your hand lower, you'd feel just how wet I am for you."

"*Fuck*, Jessa."

"Hurry up and finish your ice cream, then we can go somewhere more private."

He didn't take any more convincing, and neither did I, for that matter. We finished our ice creams in record time and headed straight back to the car.

We couldn't get enough of each other physically, but it wasn't only about the sex, despite what I told myself. Our emotional connection was growing stronger by the day. Over the time we'd spent together since I'd first stayed with the Four, both of us had been gradually uncovering the details of each other's lives, connecting us on a deeper level. No matter how ill-advised it was, since it was supposed to be a casual thing between us, and I knew that the closer we became, the more it would hurt when our arrangement inevitably ended.

We were in the middle of one of those conversations in his kitchen later that evening, learning more about each other while I prepped lasagne for everyone, and Cassius threw together a salad and homemade garlic bread.

"Did you always want to work at Alstone Holdings? Or did you feel like you have to follow that path since your family partly owns it?" Straightening up, I closed the oven door and set the timer, then hopped up onto the counter.

Cassius placed his knife down and moved to stand between my legs, his arms planted either side of me. "Both, I guess. My parents never pushed me, but they let me see the benefits of having a hand in the business." He tilted his head forwards to kiss me, gently tugging my bottom lip between his teeth. "Did your dad..."

"He didn't spell it out, but with Austin going off and doing his own thing, I definitely felt the responsibility of going into the family business." I wound my arms around his neck, shifting so that my body was aligned with his. "I don't mind, though. It's always been interesting to me, and now that his business has more or less merged with Alstone Holdings—" I cut myself off before I could mention how I'd thought about us working together, as business associates, when my mind had run away with me and I'd imagined the impossible dream of us being in a real, long-term relationship.

"Something smells good."

I disentangled myself from Cassius to see Weston peering into the oven.

"Jessa cooked for us," Cass was quick to say. "She's got many hidden talents." He flashed me a grin before leering at Weston.

West held up his hands. "I don't wanna know." Sauntering over to the fridge, he threw it open and fished out a bottle of beer before turning back to Cassius. "But going by the noises I heard from your bedroom earlier, I can imagine."

Cassius shrugged. "You could've invited yourself in. We wouldn't have minded an audience, would we?" His gaze flicked to mine, and I laughed. It was true...but not. There were times when I didn't mind an audience, enjoyed it, even, but here, with Cassius' closest friends...it was different. These were the people who knew him better than anyone. His family, not by blood, but their bond was unbreakable.

So I changed the subject. "What's the matte black thing all about? I meant to ask you before."

"Our cars?" West leaned back against the counter, his bottle of beer dangling from his fingertips.

"Yeah."

He glanced at Cassius. "Cade, wasn't it?"

Cassius nodded. "Yeah, when he got his R8. He turned up one weekend and his car was matte black, then it was Z's bike, and I was bored of my SUV colour, so..."

"Remember when Cade had Winter's car redone in matte black?"

"That's when we knew it was true luuuurve." Cassius pretended to swoon, clasping his hands over his heart.

"She didn't even know what it meant at the time." Weston shook his head. "He was so into her, it was ridiculous."

"Even when he wouldn't admit it. And he still is."

"True."

I smiled, although it was bittersweet. Caiden and Winter...I couldn't even imagine either of them being with anyone else now, especially not since I'd come to know Winter. It made me long for a relationship like that of my own, even though that had never been a priority for me before.

Glancing over at Cassius, I caught his eye, and he gave me a soft smile, which I returned.

I had to face the truth. It wasn't Caiden and Winter that had made me want a relationship.

It was *him*.

19

cassius

After hitting the contact number for Jessa's brother, I put my phone on loudspeaker while I attempted to decide which sunglasses I wanted to wear from my collection.

"Cassius." Austin's voice came through the speaker. "What's up? Is Jessa okay?"

I studied myself in a pair of mirrored aviators before pulling them off. "Yeah, she's good. Nothing's happened. I've just got a...a feeling." Pinching my brow, I paced in front of the mirror. This "feeling," whatever it was, had been getting stronger, and now it was too much to ignore. "It seems like it was almost too easy. One day Littlefinger—Petr—was threatening Jessa, the next, he was gone." I snapped my fingers. "Just like that."

A note of concern entered his voice. "If there's one thing I've learnt in business, it's that gut feelings shouldn't be ignored. Is Jessa worried?"

Shaking my head, I pulled a pair of dark sunglasses from the drawer, black on black. "Not that I know of. She seems happy, and I didn't want to bring it up with her when I don't have anything to go on other than a feeling." Satisfied with my choice in eyewear, I pushed the sunglasses up to the top of my head and closed the drawer. "What exactly went down with Li—with Petr?"

He sighed. "I guess I can tell you. Creed made enquiries with the Volkovs—who, it turned out, Ivanov was working for. It was complicated—he's related to one of them, or so I was told. I was all in favour of him having an 'accident,' but killing off the relatives of your boss's important business associates is frowned upon. Who knew?"

"He'd better not show his fucking face again."

"I've been informed that he's no longer in the country. But, fuck, if your hunch means anything, I'll make some more enquiries. That bastard isn't getting within ten feet of my sister, relative of the Volkovs or not."

"I'm with you there." Crossing over to the window, I stared out over the garden, where I knew Jessa was, although I couldn't see her from my position. "I won't let anyone touch her."

"You're a good man." His voice warmed, and a grin tugged at my lips. "I'm glad you're there for her, especially since I'm stuck here and can't watch out for her. I know how independent she is, but in times like this, it's good to know she has someone watching her back."

"Yeah, well. Uh." I cleared my throat. "Happy to be of assistance, captain. Whatever you need."

Captain? What the actual fuck?

He laughed. Loudly. "Relax, mate. You don't need to suck up to me. You're already on my good side. Don't hurt Jessa, and you'll stay there."

"Okay. Yeah. Good. Great. Brilliant."

He laughed again. Bastard. "Speak soon. We'll have

drinks. I haven't had a chance to play big-brother interrogator for one of my sister's boyfriends before."

The call disconnected with the sound of a distinctly evil laugh echoing through my room before I had a chance to reply that I wasn't Jessa's boyfriend.

Maybe for the best. I probably shouldn't tell him that I was his little sister's fuck buddy.

Leaving my phone behind, I headed down the stairs to find Jessa.

On the deck, I stopped, scanning the garden. Lena and West were over by the trees, West lying on his stomach in the shade and Lena stretched out on her back in the sun. But I bypassed them both, my eyes going straight to the girl on the sun lounger with a hand thrown over her eyes, hair piled on top of her head, and her toned, tanned body clad in a tiny mint green bikini.

"Fucking hell." I let out a strangled groan that no one was supposed to hear, but I heard Cade's snort of amusement from the chair to my left.

"You alright there, mate?"

"Fuck off. It's my natural reaction to seeing a hot girl. You're no different when you see Winter." Hopefully, my loose shorts would hide my growing boner. If they didn't, oh well. Nothing to be ashamed of here on private property. I made my way over to Jessa before he could say anything else and crouched down next to her, discreetly adjusting myself. "Jessa."

She dropped her hand and turned to look at me, her eyes hidden behind dark sunglasses. This close, she looked even better, and fuck it, I had to get my hands on her. "Roll over. Let me put sun cream on your back."

She smirked but obediently moved onto her stomach,

removing her sunglasses and burying her head in her arms. "I'm not going to say no to you getting your hands on me."

Picking up the sun lotion, I took a minute to admire the curves of her back and her ass before straddling her thighs. Drizzling some of the lotion into my palms, I placed my hands on her back.

"That's cold," she muttered, flinching away from my touch.

"Your skin's hot." Kneading her shoulders, I began to rub the lotion in. Very thoroughly, of course. My hands stroked over her back, stopping at the string of her bikini top, where I tugged lightly. "Can I?"

"Uh-huh."

Shifting on top of her, I undid her bikini top with one hand, the other trailing across her shoulders.

"Mmm." Her voice was sleepy, her body relaxing under my hands. My fingers stroked down, over her shoulder blades, and down to her sides, over the curves of her tits. My dick hardened as I slid my hands under her body, cupping the full weight of her tits. Leaning forwards, I put my mouth to her ear as I ground my cock against her.

"You're so fucking hot. Feel how hard I am?"

Something that was a cross between a laugh and a moan fell from her lips. "Don't stop."

"Are you wet, baby?" I kissed down the back of her neck, and she shivered.

"For you? Always."

There was something in her throaty murmur that had me pausing. But it couldn't be what I thought it was. Jessa was like me. She wouldn't catch feelings. This was a casual arrangement.

As I kept telling myself.

"This bikini is pointless." Shifting back, I worked my

hands down her body, stopping at the top of her ass. "It hardly covers anything. We should take it off."

"Half of it's already off."

"Then the rest should come off, too."

"Hmm. I guess it'll stop me getting tan lines." She turned her head slightly so I could see her soft, lazy smile.

"That's my girl."

Her lips curved upwards even further in reply, her eyes closed, with her lashes fanning over her cheeks.

There was no one else like Jessa.

Fuck. Fuck. *Fuck. I think I might have feelings for this girl.*

"Do you wanna take this inside?" I already knew that no one would be watching us, tucked away in our corner of the garden, while they were focused on their own things, but for some reason, I didn't want anyone to see her like this.

"Dunno, I'm feeling quite relax—*oh.*" Her words cut off as I dipped down below her bikini bottoms, smoothing my hand over her ass and down between her legs. She arched into my touch with a tiny moan.

"You were saying?"

"Fine, we'll go inside."

I helped her back into her bikini top, taking the opportunity to slide my hands all over her while I did so, then pulled her to me, keeping her body in front of my chest as we headed back to the house.

Cade smirked from behind his sunglasses as we passed him, so I threw him the middle finger. Then Jessa stumbled slightly, making her ass slam back against my dick, and I forgot everything else. I was so fucking hard for her that I couldn't even wait—the second we got into the kitchen, I pulled her across to the countertop in front of the sink.

"Here works." My mouth went to her neck as I undid

her bikini top again, then yanked down the bottoms. "Bend over, baby."

"Yesssss." She was just as into it as I was, arching her back and gripping hold of the sink. "I need you now, Cass."

"*Jessa*...fuuuuck."

My shorts were down, and my dick was pushing inside her before she even had a chance to catch her breath. The hot, slow slide as I eased inside her was incomparable. The way she gripped me so tightly as I filled her, her fingers curling over the sink, her gorgeous ass pushing back against me—it was so fucking good that I had to focus on the view out of the window over the sink so I didn't blow my load straight away.

"Harder," she panted. I gripped her hip with one hand and planted the other on the sink, caging her in, and thrust forwards, all the way in. A gasp fell from her throat, quickly followed by a sharp intake of breath.

"Weston."

"Excuse me?" I slammed into her again. And again, relishing her moans and the way she enveloped my dick in her tight, wet heat. *So fucking good.*

"Window." It came out strangled, her head falling forwards as she arched back even further.

My head flew up to see West just outside the window. He was pointedly spinning away with a hand over his face as I looked up, so I guess he'd seen what we were up to. With a grunt, I turned my attention back to the woman in front of me. "Forget him. Concentrate on how fucking good I feel inside you."

"Mmmm. So good," she moaned. "Touch me."

"Is this what you want?" I released my hold on her hip and reached forwards to cup one of her tits in my hand, rolling her nipple between my fingers as I pounded into her.

"N—ohhh. *Fuck*, Cass."

My balls were drawing up, and I knew I wasn't going to be able to hold off from coming, so I stopped playing with her lush tits and slid my fingers onto her clit. Almost as soon as I touched her, she was coming, gripping me so fucking tightly as her pussy spasmed around my cock that it was impossible to stop myself from joining her.

"Jessa, fuuuuck," I groaned, my brain going completely blank as I came down from my high. Wrapping my arm around her waist, I pulled her back against me, pressing a kiss to her head. "Fuck," I said again, my voice shaky for some reason.

"Fuck," she agreed in a whisper.

"Is it weird?"

"Is what weird?" Jessa glanced down at me. We were stretched out on the sofa, my head in her lap and my feet kicked up over the armrest, while the TV played *Black Widow* in the background.

"Being here after everything. The whole thing."

She stared into space as her fingers raked through my hair, her nails scratching over my scalp. Eventually, she replied. "It is and it isn't. I feel like I've changed a lot. After Portia left...I'm not blaming her for the way I was, because that was all on me, but I think that us growing apart gave me perspective that I didn't have before." Her mouth twisted, and then she sighed. "I guess...I... All I can do is move forwards and hope that people realise that my past actions aren't a reflection of who I am now. You know?"

Raising my head, I moved into a sitting position. "Babe. Let me tell you something. Anyone who defines you by your past doesn't know the real you. You're fucking amazing, inside and out."

Her eyes widened, and her mouth fell open.

"Yeah, I mean it," I said emphatically before she could ask the inevitable question.

She swallowed hard, her eyes looking suddenly glassy, so I tugged her onto my lap so she was straddling me. Her breath hit my lips, and then we were kissing, long and slow and so fucking good.

"I think I'm addicted to your mouth," I said when we finally drew apart. That brought a smile to her face.

"Same, to yours."

"You..." Words I never meant to say, words I didn't even know were inside of me, came out of my mouth in a rush. "I like this. I don't have to be switched on. I can just be me with you."

Cupping my cheek, she stared at me, confused. "You're you with the others, aren't you?"

"Yeah..." I attempted to articulate my thoughts. "I am. They're my best friends, and they know me better than anyone else. I guess sometimes I feel like I have to be the one making the conversation lighter, y'know?"

Her thumb stroked across my jaw. "I think so."

"Don't get me wrong. I'm funny as fuck." I shrugged. "But sometimes I might wanna be moody like Cade, or whatever, but people look to me to cheer shit up."

"With great power comes great responsibility," she said solemnly.

My grin stretched across my face. "Did you just Spider-Man me, babe?"

"Maybe." A smile curved over her lips. Leaning forwards, she kissed me softly. "But seriously, I do get what you're saying. You...me...whatever this is...you can always be yourself with me. Happy, sad, angry, whatever."

There was that weird feeling in my chest again, and this time I dealt with it by wrapping my arms around her and stroking my lips across hers.

Yeah. I was addicted to her mouth.

And maybe some other parts of her, too.

20

jessa

The morning started like any other. I didn't suspect anything, and why would I? Movies and books teach us that the bad men come at night, wrapped in darkness and hidden in the shadows.

It didn't happen that way for me.

The sun shone brightly, a light breeze in the air carrying the tang of salt from the sea. Curled up on my sofa, I sipped my mug of tea while I browsed social media. Cassius' social media, to be exact. My finger traced over his latest image, posted last night, captionless except for a single fire emoji.

It was me.

My stomach flipped, a smile spreading across my face. He must've taken it the previous night without me noticing because I was silhouetted in the doorway of his house, right as I was leaving. My body was completely in shadow, so no one would have known it was me. Except...he'd tagged me in the image.

My social media had been locked down since everything that had happened at the docks, but there were enough people that knew us both. I told myself not to read the comments, but I couldn't help myself. Thankfully, they were mostly speculation, since no one else knew about our exclusive fuck buddy agreement, and although I knew we'd been seen kissing at the beach party, we'd actually hung out separately for most of it.

There was no reason for me to get my hopes up anyway, despite the image, and yet, my smile remained, thoughts of Cassius occupying every corner of my mind.

To stop my wayward thoughts, I opened up my messages to a group chat I'd been added to on the day of the party. This one consisted of Winter, Kinslee, Lena, Lena's friend Raine, and me. The emotions that had come over me when I'd been included... I cleared my throat to get rid of the sudden lump that formed. It was something so simple, yet the fact that they'd chosen to include me filled me with happiness and belonging.

From what I could work out, Raine designed clothing and had made Lena some trousers that the other girls were raving about. Even though I'd only just been added to the chat, they'd made sure to explain everything to me, sending a million pictures and descriptions and tagging me in almost every message. I tapped out a reply to the latest string of messages, which had come through last night when I was with Cassius, before resting my head on the back of my sofa and finishing up my tea with a smile on my face.

A loud buzzing sound interrupted the peaceful quiet inside my flat, and I answered the intercom with a bounce in my step.

"Flower delivery," a gruff voice said through the speaker.

Glancing out of the open window, I saw a white delivery van idling at the kerb, large flowers painted along the side along with the company name and phone number. "Thanks, I'll be down in a second." Smiling, I took the stairs two at a time, keys in hand, leaving my phone in my apartment. At the building door, I was greeted by a huge bunch of flowers in every colour of the rainbow clasped in the delivery guy's arms.

The first flowers that I'd ever been sent, and they were *beautiful.*

My smile widened. Surely there was only one person who would have sent them...

The delivery guy thrust the blooms at me, then shoved an electronic pad in my face for me to sign. I couldn't even see, not with the masses of flowers obscuring my vision, so I carefully placed them on the apartment front steps before turning back to the guy to sign the pad.

Fuck.

A scream tore from my throat, instantly cut off by the hand that clamped over my mouth and nose. My struggles were ineffectual as another hand came around my neck, crushing my windpipe.

My vision swam, spots dancing in front of my eyes.

The last thing I saw before everything went black was the cruel, twisting smile of Petr Ivanov.

When I came to, I was disorientated for a moment, blinking slowly, before everything came back to me in a rush. Panic engulfed me, my vision darkening again as my heart rate shot up, and I struggled to catch my breath. Instinctively, I opened my mouth to scream, but all that came out was a hoarse scraping noise. I struggled, unable to move, desperately working to get air into my lungs.

A laugh came from over to my left. The sudden sound sliced through my panic, shocking my brain into action, and for the first time since I'd regained consciousness, I focused on my breathing, actively working to slow it, counting in my head. Once it was a little more under control, I turned my head to see Petr Ivanov, sitting on a metal chair, watching me. He laughed again when our eyes met but remained where he was, his pose casual, his arms resting on his thighs. One hand played with a black object that I couldn't make out from my position, and in the other, he held a phone.

I have to get out of here.

Slowly, I turned my head away from Petr, listening hard in case he moved, and scanned my surroundings, growing more desperate as I took in the bare room. I was in what looked like some kind of empty storage facility, with a dirty floor and walls and high, cracked windows. There was only one door that I could see, and it was tightly closed. I'd been tied to a chair, my ankles immobile and my wrists bound behind my back.

I had nothing on me. I hadn't even brought my phone with me, and I had no idea what had happened to my keys —probably dropped back at my apartment building. My clothes were completely impractical, too—a thin green summer dress and gold flip-flops. It had been a warm morning, but in here it was already cool with a breeze blowing from somewhere behind me. I shivered, pulling at the restraints that bound me so tightly, but they didn't even budge.

Hot, frustrated tears filled my eyes, and I yanked at the ropes again, only succeeding in making the rough, scratchy material dig into my skin, rubbing it raw in places. Stifling a whimper, I bit down on my lip, refusing to let Petr have the satisfaction of getting a reaction out of me.

"Wh-what do you want?" I managed to scrape out, meeting his hard, flinty gaze again.

Pocketing the phone, he stood, crossing the short distance and coming to a stop in front of me. He stared down at me, his mouth twisted into a sneer. I held his gaze, refusing to be cowed, even though fear was choking me, thick and heavy, as I sat helplessly bound before him.

His eyes narrowed as he looked at me with pure hatred in his gaze. My breath caught in my throat as he lifted his hand, revealing the black object, which I could now see was a metallic oblong. He pressed something on it, and a silver blade flicked out of the end, the serrated edge gleaming in the dim light that penetrated the grimy, cracked windows.

"You ruined my life. Now, I ruin yours."

21

cassius

The sound of my phone woke me. Without opening my eyes, I fumbled for it, swiping the screen to answer. "Hello?"

"Cassius."

I was instantly awake at the sound of Austin's voice. "What's up?"

His low, angry tone came through the speaker. "It seems we were misinformed. Ivanov is still in the country. He was staying with one of the contacts of the Volkovs, but last night he disappeared."

"Fuck. You think he's on his way here?"

"I don't know. Probably not, but can you—"

"I'm on my way to Jessa's right now," I assured him, already out of bed and pulling on my clothes. There was no way I was leaving her alone if he was still around.

"Good. It's just my luck I'm in fucking Edinburgh visiting suppliers, but I'll make some more enquiries my end, see if I can find out anything else. Keep me updated."

"Will do." Disconnecting the call, I ran downstairs, stopping only to shove my feet into my trainers and grab my car keys. The feeling I'd had, the fucking premonition I'd ignored, was now a warning siren blaring in my head. Something was wrong. Badly wrong.

I made it to Jessa's in record time, parking on the double yellow lines and slamming my hand on the buzzer over and over again. There was no answer.

"Fuck!" I shouted, yanking my phone from my pocket and hitting West's number. As soon as it started ringing, I scanned the names next to the other door buzzers, then pressed the buzzer for James Granville.

"Cass." Weston answered at the same time as James' "hello" came from the intercom.

"Hang on, West." I spoke into the intercom. "James, it's Cassius. I'm here to see Jessa, but she's not answering. Can you let me up?"

She has to be asleep. Her car's still here.

Even as I told myself that, I knew I was already too late.

James buzzed me into the building, and I gave West a rundown of the situation as I headed up the stairs to Jessa's apartment.

"I'm pulling up the security footage now," he told me as I hammered on Jessa's door to no reply. There was silence for a few minutes, and then I heard his sharp intake of breath. "Fuck. It's Littlefinger—I'd know that fucker anywhere. He just got out of a white van..." There was a clicking sound. "Okay, zoomed in. The van says 'Rosie's Blooms.' I'm sending you the phone number on the van and the number plate too."

I held my breath as he continued to relay everything he was seeing on the screen.

"He's carrying some flowers to the building. I can't see him now without switching cameras to the one that faces the building, but let's watch the rest of this one—*shit*. He's got Jessa. He's...dragging her to the van... Now he's driving away."

I'd heard enough.

Littlefinger had my girl, and I was going to make very fucking sure he regretted it.

After a quick call to the flower shop, which just had a recorded message saying that it was open at 10:00 a.m., I had West and Lena scouring the feeds of the surrounding roads, trying to see if we could pin down Littlefinger's destination. Thank fuck there was so much CCTV around, and since we had a timestamp for the video outside her apartment, we could check the live feeds for the surrounding roads. Running back to my car, I called Austin to let him know what was going on. There was no answer, so I left a voicemail, then for lack of any other options, input the flower shop address into my satnav and started up my SUV.

The shop had a south London address, and every single one of my instincts told me that this was where I needed to be.

Hitting the accelerator, I set off.

When I pulled up outside the shop, it was just opening up, an older woman with grey curls and glasses setting out a flower display in front of the large window.

"Morning." I flashed her a grin, calling on all my skills to appear my usual charming self, even though I was ready to rip someone's head off.

"Morning, dear." She returned my smile. "How can I help you today?"

Getting straight to the point, I brought up the subject of

the van, coming up with some bollocks story about how it had dented my sister's car, reading out the number plate and asking if it was registered to the shop. Frowning, she nodded slowly.

"That's our spare van. We use it at the weekends and busy times of the year, but it's kept in the car park down there normally." She pointed at a tiny road that ran between two tall buildings. "Are you sure that this was the van that hit your sister's car? It's not due to be used today."

Thinking fast, I shook my head. "It all happened so quickly. My sister might have written the number plate down wrong. Is it a plain white van?"

A look of relief came over her face. "Oh, ours is white, but it has our logo on the sides. Large flowers—you can't miss them."

I widened my smile. "Phew. In that case, we have the wrong van. I'm sorry to bother you. Thank you for your time."

"Good luck in finding the culprit, dear." She tutted. "Drivers today! Too many people in a hurry, that's the problem."

"True." With a smile and a nod, I left her, getting back into my SUV. I continued down the road so I could find somewhere to turn around, calling West again using my Bluetooth connection to give him the latest update. The bloody Bluetooth wouldn't connect to begin with, but after I punched my dashboard a couple of times, it decided to work.

"Cass?" West answered as I was executing a perfect three-point turn in a side street.

"Did you know that Bluetooth was named after a Viking king?"

"What the fuck are you on about?"

Focus. "Never mind. So the van belongs to the flower people, but they said it's not supposed to be in use today. It's kept in a car park—I'm heading there now, but can you pull up any feeds around the place?"

"I'll see what I can do. There might not be any, so leave your phone on. I've got your tracker up on the screen so I can see where you are."

Back out on the main road, I headed back past the flower shop again and indicated to turn down the road that the woman had pointed out.

"Stupid fucking side streets. I'd better not scrape my car," I muttered, wincing as I squeezed between the buildings.

"Cass? I've located the car park, and guess what. It's right behind the hotel Littlefinger was staying in."

"I thought I recognised the area."

"Cass?" Caiden's voice was suddenly on the line. "If you see the van, don't go running into shit. We're on our way if it's confirmed that he's there, so wait for us. Z's contacting Creed, too, since he's closer than we are."

"Yeah," I said distractedly, reaching the end of the lane. It opened into a private parking area surrounded by a chain-link fence and a barrier entry. Right in front of me, parked directly opposite where I'd stopped, was the van. "It's here."

"On our way. Don't move until we get there." Caiden ended the call.

Fuck that. I wasn't about to hang around, not when Jessa was in danger. Continuing past the car park and out onto the other side, I drove down the street until I found an open parking space. Once I was parked, I called Austin again, and this time he answered, sounding out of breath.

"Any news?"

"I've found the van. I know she's here somewhere."

He let out a string of swear words. "I'm on my way to the airport, getting the first flight home. I've left a message for Creed, and I'll keep trying him until I get an answer." His voice cracked. "Don't let anything happen to her."

"I won't," I promised, hoping he could hear the conviction in my tone.

After removing my sunglasses, I exited the car, and slid my phone into my pocket, making sure the tracking was still on. I forced myself to wait for a minute. My boys weren't with me, but that didn't mean I was helpless. I was Cassius motherfucking Drummond, and I'd make sure that Littlefinger would regret the day he stepped foot in Alstone.

Still, it would be helpful to have a gun right about now. Or a knife. Or even a slingshot. Fuck, I'd take a fountain pen at this point.

Then I remembered the folding mini shovel that was kept in my glovebox with the emergency supplies. It was supposed to be there if I ever needed to dig the car out of mud or snow or something—I'd never even looked at it before now. But if shovels were good enough to take out zombies in *The Walking Dead*, then maybe they'd be good enough for me.

I hoped.

Grabbing the shovel, I unfolded it and clasped it in my hand, attempting to look natural in case anyone wondered what I was doing. Rummaging in the boot, I found a wrench and the forgotten bolt cutters that had been lying in the car ever since the last time I'd used them, when we were taking down an illegal dog-fighting ring.

Now I was fucking ready. Who needed a gun or knives when you had rusty bolt cutters, a wrench, and a small shovel?

As inconspicuously as I could, I made my way to the car park and ducked under the barrier. There were two cameras, but I had to take my chances. First of all, I peered inside the van, which was empty except for a few bunches of flowers. That ruled that out. Clenching my jaw, I scanned the buildings around me, my eyes coming to rest on a dilapidated, taped-up four-storey building on the far left that looked like it was partway through demolition. One side of it was torn away, covered in plastic sheeting that flapped in the breeze. My gaze passed over it as I continued to scan the area, then slid back to it.

Pulling out my phone again, I ducked down behind the van, out of view of the cameras, and called Weston back to let him know what I'd found.

"We're on our way with the drone, so we can try for a heat signal in the building then—it might pick something up. From what I can tell, the building was a car park and storage facility, but it's being pulled down."

"Yeah, I got that," I told him. "Do you think she could be in any of the other buildings?"

"They're all legit businesses, from what I can tell, except for the brown building with the black windows— that one's apartments."

"Hmm." I thought about it. "My gut feeling is the demolition building, but I guess the apartments are possible."

"There's the hotel he was staying in, too," he reminded me.

"Yeah, but getting Jessa inside it without attracting attention might be difficult."

"Good point."

"Okay. I'm gonna try the demo building while I'm waiting for you."

"Don't do anything without us. Cade will fucking kill you, and so will I if anything happens to you," my best mate warned me, his tone hard.

"It's okay." A grim smile twisted across my lips as I tapped my shovel with the tip of the bolt cutters. "I have my zombie killers with me."

"*What?*"

"Yeah, bye." I ended the call because we had no time to waste, and if I stopped to think about everything that could go wrong, my head wouldn't be clear enough to face whatever waited for me. Squaring my shoulders resolutely, I headed for the demolition building.

22

jessa

"How did I ruin your life?" My throat was so sore, but I forced the words out in a hoarse, cracked voice. My only option was to keep Petr talking in the hope that I could buy myself some time. No one knew where I was, so maybe it was pointless, but I wasn't about to lie down and take whatever he had planned for me.

Instead of answering, he crouched down in front of me. Lifting his hand, he placed the tip of the knife to my thigh and pressed down before drawing away. A gasp fell from my throat at the sudden sting, a bubble of blood appearing where he'd cut me.

"How?" I whispered again, whimpering as his other hand came to my cut thigh, his fingers digging into my flesh as he bared his teeth at me in a snarl.

"Whore. You *ruined* me."

"What did I do?" My fear was temporarily overridden as I stared at him, racking my brain for what I could have done that would have been so bad that it had drawn him to this.

"You ruined me," he repeated, spitting out the words through bared teeth. Gesturing to his crotch with the knife, he snarled something that I didn't know the meaning of —*kastrirovala*—but a memory flashed through my mind, and a dawning horror came over me.

The photo he'd sent.

The bloody screwdriver object.

The way I'd wildly jabbed it up, and his agonised howl as it had pierced easily through his jeans and into his flesh.

Guilt like I'd never felt before raged inside me, warring with the voice in my head that insisted he'd brought this on himself.

A choked sob fell from my throat, tearing painfully at my abused vocal cords, but I couldn't stop it. Was this my punishment? Was this how it would end?

The tears came thick and fast as he continued to snarl words at me, his gaze filled with retribution. Standing, his hands went to the button of his jeans, and he yanked them down in a quick, jerky movement.

My jaw dropped.

I stared in horror, helpless to look away, facing the evidence of my panicked movements that night at the docks. Instead of the normal...equipment...there was a misshapen stump—a mess of angry red scarring... My heartbeat pounded in my ears, drowning out the sound of my panicked breaths, my brain unable to process just how awful it looked—

The punch came out of nowhere, directly into my midsection. Gasping, I curled my body instinctively, jerking back when my bound arms stopped my movement. Pain throbbed through my body, filling me until I couldn't even breathe, or think, or do anything except remain frozen in place. Another punch, and I heard a crack, and a sharp, agonising burst of pain swept through me, starting at my ribs and radiating outwards.

He laughed at my choked whimper.

Through the haze of burning agony, I dimly registered a loud *clang* coming from somewhere and Petr's footsteps heading away from me. Holding myself very, very still, I closed my eyes and took an unsteady breath. Then another. Then another, my lungs burning with every inhale and exhale.

There was a rustling sound, like plastic sheeting being moved. "He is here for you." The amusement in Petr's voice pierced through my consciousness. "He came alone. Stupid boy."

Instantly, I knew who he was talking about.

Cassius.

I had to protect him.

Fear for the man I'd fallen for overtook the pain, shocking my body with a burst of sudden adrenaline.

Opening my eyes, I stared straight at Petr.

"*No*," I rasped. "Don't...hurt...him."

His gaze flew to mine, his flinty eyes narrowing and his lips twisting into a mocking sneer. I vaguely noticed that he'd pulled his jeans back up, and that was something I was more than grateful for, because I was struggling to even speak right now, and if I was confronted with the evidence again...

Cassius. His gorgeous, smiling face came into my mind, and it gave me the strength to push the words out. "Please. I'll...do anything. *Anything.*"

"You would give yourself for the boy?" Surprise flashed in his gaze before it was replaced with a cold, calculating look.

I nodded once. I no longer noticed the tears that fell or the hurt that encompassed every part of me. All of that was unimportant. Nothing mattered except keeping Cassius safe.

Because I loved him.

"Stay quiet, and do not move. When he reaches us, I will incapacitate him—"

The panicked noise that came from my throat gave him pause, and he shook his head, a short, impatient movement. "I will not harm him. I will allow us time to leave. And you will willingly agree to be mine, *suka*. Mine to break, until you cannot be repaired."

Crossing back over to me, he gripped my throat, squeezing until my vision swam. "Yes?"

"Yes," I choked out with the last of my breath.

"It is done." He released me, and precious air filled my lungs.

The adrenaline drained from my body in a rush. As long as Cassius was okay, I could handle it. Even if I wasn't going to make it out alive.

My eyes fell shut.

Darkness came, swift and blissful.

23

cassius

By the time my fingers closed around the handle of the fifth door, I was beginning to regret bringing the bolt cutters and the shovel. Carrying one in each hand was fine, but two in one hand wasn't ideal. Shifting my grip, I swung the door open.

I had about five seconds to scan the room.

It was long enough.

Five...a long trail through the thick layer of building dust on the floor, with footprints at regular intervals, like someone had been dragged into the room.

Four...the whole side of the room was missing, covered with the plastic sheeting that I'd seen from the outside.

Three...two chairs in the centre of the room, facing away from the missing wall.

Two...a girl, slumped in one of the chairs, eyes closed, her head lolling to the side.

One...a flash of silver and a dark shadow.

My body reacted on instinct, fuelled by the rage that burned a white-hot path through my veins. Dropping my hold on the door and gripping onto the shovel and bolt cutters in both hands, I twisted my body and swung out. There was no time to think, but I *knew* I had to do it.

Everything happened so fucking quickly.

A loud curse word that definitely wasn't in English, then a body slamming into mine, followed by a slashing pain across my side.

The bolt cutters fell from my grip as I was knocked to the floor. Blinking, I climbed to my feet, my eyes taking in the scene in front of me in an instant. Littlefinger, also clambering to his feet, a knife clutched in one hand and the other grasping his thigh where there was a gash in his jeans, a dark red stain seeping through. I allowed myself a second of satisfaction as I stood up straight.

"You're going down, fucker." I grinned, without humour for once, but with the knowledge that he was about to pay for what he'd done.

He lunged at me with the knife, but I was ready with my zombie killer shovel.

I swung it.

It connected with his head with a loud, satisfying *thunk*, and he dropped to the floor like a stone.

Without even wasting another breath, I ran across the room to where Jessa was tied to the chair and let the shovel fall from my fingers. Smoothing her hair back from her face, I gripped her chin in my hand. "Jessa?"

She looked so fucking small and fragile.

And she wasn't waking up. Why wasn't she waking up?

"Jessa!" Fuck, why couldn't I think?

I placed my hand against her chest and felt it. The slight rise and fall, shallow but there. She was alive. I wasn't too late.

My eyes fucking stung.

"Jessa, wake up. Fuck, *please*." Dropping to the floor, I

went to clasp her hand in mine, and that's when I realised she was tied to the chair. Why hadn't I noticed?

My fingers betrayed me, shaking too much to undo the knots. With a groan, I tore myself away, running back to my discarded bolt cutters and swiping them from the floor. With a quick glance at Littlefinger to make sure he was still out cold, I raced back over to Jessa and carefully cut her free, finally managing to untie the bonds. Her wrists and ankles had been rubbed raw, and there was a trail of blood running down her leg from a spot on her upper thigh. My gaze tracked over her body, a red haze of anger descending as I took in the darkening bruising around her throat and thigh. If I hadn't got here when I had...

I swallowed the lump in my throat. Carefully, so fucking carefully, I lifted her into my arms and sank to the floor. A whimper of pain tore from her.

"Jessa?"

"C-Cass?" Her voice was so hoarse that I could barely make out what she was saying. Gritting my teeth against the rage that flared up again, I kept my attention on her. Her lashes fluttered, and then she slowly blinked her eyes open and looked up at me.

My breath caught in my throat. The green was dulled, the whites of her eyes shot through with red. Her skin had paled beneath her tan, and her normally pouty, soft lips were cracked and almost colourless.

She gave a slow, heaving breath, her body shuddering against mine. "Petr?"

"I took care of him." Even though I tried to keep my voice soft, it came out as an enraged growl. "That fucking bastard deserved so much more than being knocked out by my zombie killer."

The tiniest of smiles tugged at her lips, and there was an ache in my chest. "Zom—"

"Yeah," I interrupted to save her from talking when she was in so much pain. "My shovel. Doubles up as a zombie killer, or in this case, to knock out—"

A small scraping sound was the only warning I had, but my instincts were on point today, and I lifted Jessa off me, pushing her behind me and spinning around in a crouch. Littlefinger was lunging at me, knife in the air, and my shovel was too far to reach.

The wrench.

I yanked it from my pocket and threw my arm out, connecting with his shin as hard as I could. A howl came from him, and then there was another noise from behind him as he fell into me—shouts and running footsteps.

His weight was only on me for a couple of seconds before it was gone.

When I looked up, Creed was standing there, extending a hand to me.

Climbing to my feet, I turned away from Littlefinger, trusting Creed to deal with it. The only thing that mattered right now was making sure that Jessa was okay.

"Wait." He stopped me with a hand on my arm. "Watch what happens. You'll both want to see this."

My gaze slid back to Littlefinger and the tall, grey-haired man in the black suit that was standing in front of him. I nodded and made my way back over to Jessa. She'd actually climbed to her feet, and although she was gripping onto the back of the chair, holding herself unnaturally still, I was so fucking proud of her. Defiance that I thought might have died gleamed in her eyes as her gaze focused on Littlefinger, the green brighter again, and that ache in my chest grew, impossible to ignore.

I carefully curled my arm around her waist, drawing back when I heard her hiss of pain. "It's okay," she whispered. "J-just bruised."

Before I could reply, her attention was caught by the man standing in front of Littlefinger. His features were harsh, his face showing no expression as he spoke to Littlefinger in Russian, shaking his head at Littlefinger's replies. When Littlefinger gestured towards us, Jessa's breath hitched, and I placed my hand over the top of hers, curving it over the metal chair back. She leaned into me, swaying slightly on her feet but letting me support her, and I breathed out a sigh of relief.

"I think that's one of the Volkovs," I murmured to Jessa. "You know, Creed's business associates. The ones that were connected to Petr."

She didn't reply, focused on the conversation between the two men. Now that she was standing here, everything in me wanted to go over and take another swing at Littlefinger, to hurt him until he was begging for mercy. To make him pay for what he'd done to Jessa.

But I didn't have to.

Littlefinger's voice grew louder and pleading, his hands gesturing in the air, while the Volkov guy remained impassive in front of him. Creed stood just to the side of the two of them, his pose deceptively casual, but I recognised the coiled tension in him, ready to act at any moment.

Volkov moved so fast I almost missed it. A casual, graceful flick of his hand, and a blade sliced along Littlefinger's throat from left to right, quick and precise. Blood began spurting out as shock entered Littlefinger's eyes, grasping at his throat with a look of complete disbelief on his face.

He fell to the ground, blood pouring from beneath his

fingers, and Volkov turned his back in one final, deliberate movement. Next to him, Creed pulled out a tissue from his pocket and calmly dabbed the flecks of blood that had hit his cheek. After dropping the tissue onto Littlefinger's now unmoving body, he smiled, slow and satisfied. Leaning across to Volkov, he said something too low for me to hear, to which Volkov nodded, then disappeared from the room.

Creed tapped out something on his phone before looking up again. "Clean-up crew are on their way." He raised his voice, directing his attention towards me and Jessa, so I nodded in acknowledgement.

"It's over now." I placed a kiss to the top of her head, and she made a tiny noise that sounded like a sob.

Fuck.

It tore me open.

"Jessa, I—" My sentence was left unfinished because the door was bursting open, and Caiden and Zayde were piling into the room.

Jessa stiffened in my arms, moving slightly, and I winced at the sudden pain in my side.

What the fuck? Drawing back from her enough to see properly, I looked down at myself.

It was at that point I realised that there was a line of blood seeping through the fabric of my T-shirt.

24

jessa

"That fucker better not have ruined my favourite T-shirt." Cassius unwound his arm from around me, holding on to make sure I was still standing before he let go. "Okay?" he asked softly, and I nodded once, even though I felt like my legs were about to give way. My fingers gripped the cold metal of the back of the chair as I concentrated on breathing slowly, staying as still as possible. I was fairly sure that at least one of my ribs was cracked, because any movement would send a shooting pain through them.

"Fine. Go to them," I croaked. He shot me a concerned look, but I nodded at him, and he sighed.

"Are you—"

"Go. I'm sure."

His fingers trailed over the back of my hand. "Promise I'll be right back." Stepping away from me, he pulled his T-shirt over his head as he made his way over to his friends. He glanced back at me, and I attempted a smile. That seemed to be enough to reassure him because after one final, concerned glance, he turned his attention to Caiden and Zayde.

Closing my eyes, I refocused on my breathing. In. Out. Slow and steady.

"It's just a scratch," Caiden was saying. I opened my eyes to see him examining Cassius' side. "No deeper than the cuts on your thumbs you cried about."

"Fuck off." The humour was back in Cassius' voice, and the relief that filled me brought tears to my eyes. He was okay. Littlefinger was gone, for good this time, and Cassius was okay.

As the tears obscured my vision, my head started pounding and I suddenly needed air. I felt like I was suffocating in here, my lungs burning and my ribs on fire. Uncurling my fingers from the chair, I took a tiny, experimental step. There was a shooting pain, and I hugged my arms to my chest to support my ribs. This time when I took a step, the pain was slightly more bearable. Keeping my pace slow and as steady as possible, pausing after every step, I started making my way towards the door.

"What the fuck were you thinking, running in here like that? I told you to wait." That was Caiden's voice again, low, letting the anger bleed through his tone now he'd ascertained that Cassius wasn't injured.

There was silence for a second, and then as I glanced over at the boys, I saw Cassius' jaw set as he met Caiden's eyes. "You would've done the same. Any of us would have. If one of our friends was in danger and we could do something, we wouldn't leave them. Even if it was someone we didn't know, we'd still help, right?" His eyes narrowed, and after a moment, Caiden nodded, accepting his words.

"You're right. I would've. We would've." He squeezed

Cassius' shoulder, and Cassius gave him a small, genuine smile in return.

Almost at the door, I looked at Cassius, standing there with his friends, who were studying his wound and asking him questions—still angry at him for rushing into danger —and I knew what I had to do.

Turning away from him, I met Creed's gaze. As he lowered his phone from his ear, his golden eyes scrutinised me, and he inclined his head slightly before stepping closer.

"Can you take me...?" My voice trailed off, hoarse and scratchy. I needed to leave before anyone noticed, before they tried to speak to me and realised that I was hurt. They'd either give me misplaced sympathy, or even worse, Cassius might feel guilty for not being able to get to me before anything happened. And I wouldn't let that happen. There was no way that I wanted him hurting in any way. He was far too important to me. Of course, Caiden and Zayde might just redirect their anger towards me—anger because I'd managed to put Cassius in this situation. And they'd have every right to be angry. He could have been hurt so much worse than a shallow cut.

He could have died if the knife had gone in deeper.

A shuddering breath escaped me, and I pleaded with Creed silently.

His gaze flicked between me and Cassius, and he sighed, shaking his head. "You shouldn't run away."

"Please."

"This isn't the right decision," he said softly, but he held out his hand, and I took it.

We escaped unnoticed.

"Where does it hurt?" he asked when I was settled in the cool leather interior of his car.

Leaning my head against the window, I noticed Winter,

Lena, and Weston running across the car park, and I let out a breath, glad that Cassius would have all of his friends with him. He needed them now, I knew that.

What he didn't need was me—a girl who was only supposed to be a fuck buddy, but who had not only managed to stupidly go and fall in love with him despite the warnings I'd constantly given myself, but worst of all, had put his life in danger. If he hadn't been able to defend himself, if Creed and the other guy hadn't turned up when they did...

"My ribs." I desperately tried to ignore the other pain, just for a moment. The pain that was worse than the physical. The physical pain would be gone, I knew, once I had medicine and rest. But the pain inside me...that would take a lot longer to heal.

Creed nodded as if he'd expected that answer. "I'll take you to my private doctor, then we'll take it from there. Austin's plane should be here soon, and he'll want to see you."

"Thank you," I whispered as his car started up, taking me away from the nightmare scene.

Taking me away from Cassius.

"Seriously, mate, I wish someone had been videoing it. I was like a ninja—" I stopped mid-sentence as my best mate shot through the doorway and threw himself at me, followed in quick succession by my sister and Winter.

"Why don't you have a top on?"

Ignoring Lena's question and the face she was pulling, I met Winter's eyes. "Can you check on Jessa?"

She nodded instantly, and I smiled. My smile dropped when she frowned at me.

"Uh, Cass? Where is she?"

"*What?*" Barely able to disguise the sudden panic in my voice, I spun around to face the chair.

It was empty.

There was no sign of Jessa, or Creed, for that matter. Just a body on the floor, blood pooling on either side of the neck area.

"Creed's taken her." Zayde held up his phone. "Gone to get her checked out. Her brother's on his way to her now."

"What did he do to her?" Winter interrupted. Her blue eyes were wide and troubled.

"He...uh." The fucking lump in my throat was back, and I was suddenly conscious of everyone staring at me. Clearing my throat, I tried again, the image of Jessa, limp and bound to the chair, forever burned into my mind. "She had bruises on her thigh. A, uh, a knife cut there as well. And bruises all around her throat." I growled out the next words. "She could hardly fucking speak."

There were general noises of anger and distress from everyone around me, and I knew right then that they'd accepted Jessa. Something inside me settled, although I couldn't say what it was.

"I need to see her," I muttered, quiet enough that no one caught my words.

"Give her time with her brother."

Okay, someone caught my words. Glancing down at Lena, I nodded, understanding passing between us. She gave me a soft, almost sad look, and I knew she was thinking of her confession to me not so long ago. I pulled her into a hug, wrapping my arms around her, and she managed to not even comment on the fact that I didn't have a T-shirt on, hugging me back tightly.

"Love you," I murmured into her hair.

"Love you, too." She released me, and West was there, pulling her into his arms. He mouthed, *I've got her*, and I shot him a smile, then turned to Z, because all this emotion was too much. Especially now Jessa wasn't here.

And I really didn't want to think about that right now.

"Have you ever knocked someone out with a shovel?"

Zayde raised a brow but said nothing.

"If it's good enough for a zombie, it's good enough for a human."

"Zombies are humans," West interjected.

"Undead humans. Can you even call them humans? They've lost all their humanity, surely?" Winter pursed her lips, deep in thought, causing Cade to laugh and drag her into his arms, kissing her cheek. Here I was, third-wheeling again. Well, me and Z. And Littlefinger. Although I guess that didn't count, since he was dead.

Although...

"Hey, if someone was going to come back as a ghost, would it happen straight away?" I stared at his body, then glanced back at the others, catching Cade's eye.

"How the fuck would I know? Do I look like the ghost expert?" He shook his head at me, managing to look disdainful and disapproving all at once.

"I wasn't asking you specifically. I was asking everyone in general."

"I think I can safely say that none of us are experts on the paranormal, mate." West gave me a quick grin over the top of Lena's head. "So based on my totally made-up knowledge, I'm gonna say it happens straight away."

"Can we change the subject, please? At least back to zombies." Winter shivered, frowning in the direction of Littlefinger's body. The clean-up crew showed up just as we were debating whether a crossbow or a katana would be better for taking out the undead, and we got out of there. I was more than happy to leave that place behind.

Once I was back in my SUV, Winter joined me. She'd arrived with Lena and Weston in Lena's car, while Caiden and Z had taken Cade's Audi R8. I could tell she had something on her mind, but I waited for her to bring it up.

We sat in silence for a while, but once we were on the motorway and heading back towards Alstone, she finally spoke, her voice soft.

"How are you doing, Cass? Really?"

"I'm fine."

There was no reply, but a slim hand slid onto my arm.

I sighed in defeat.

"Okay, I'm worried about Jessa." Once I'd started talking, I couldn't stop. "Fuck, Winter. I was so scared for her, and when I saw Littlefinger, I wanted to fucking kill him for what he'd done to her. She looked—" My voice cracked, and the hand on my arm tightened, Winter's thumb rubbing in soothing circles. "I've never seen anyone like that before. Remember how you were in the hospital?"

Winter nodded.

"Yeah, well, it was too much like that for my liking, except she wasn't safe right then. He was right fucking there, and he'd done all this shit to her, and-and—" I broke off with a frustrated noise, slamming my hand down on the steering wheel. "She had all these bruises around her throat, and there was blood, and—"

"Hey. Breathe." Winter ran her hand up and down my arm. "It's okay now. She's safe. Creed's got her, and so's her brother. Littlefinger is really, properly dead this time..." Her voice trailed off, and I could feel her eyes on the side of my face as I stared at the road. Silence fell for about thirty seconds before she added, "And no, he's not coming back as a ghost."

I shot her a glance, noticing the corners of her lips turning up, and I laughed. "It's probably not very likely, yeah?"

"I'd say so."

"I fucking love you, by the way."

She beamed at me. "Same."

There was silence until we reached the outskirts of Alstone, when she spoke again. "I'm assuming you're planning on sending Jessa a text when you get back, or a voicemail or something, so she knows you're there. Ready for whatever comes next."

"Yeah, of course I am. I'm not gonna sit around waiting to hear from her when I'm this worried about her. But 'whatever comes next?'" I repeated her words, unsure of what she meant.

"Yeah. You'll work it out."

"Work what out? Stop being so cryptic."

She just laughed and refused to answer.

"Really fucking helpful," I mumbled, taking the turning that led onto our road.

What *was* coming next? Whatever it was, I had no fucking clue.

Hopefully, it involved Jessa getting better and zero people out to get us. I wanted to enjoy the remainder of my last summer as a student.

Fingers crossed.

25

jessa

The next week passed in a bit of a blur. After I'd been checked over by the doctor, I'd been informed that I'd cracked a rib and another two were bruised—or more accurately, Petr had done that to me—so I spent a lot of time resting.

In London. With my brother.

If anything good could come out of this mess, it was that Austin and I were actually having proper, deep conversations like we'd never had before. Like I'd said to Cassius previously, Austin had moved out when he was eighteen and I was fourteen, and what eighteen-year-old guy wants to hang out with their annoying teenage sister? Maybe some did, but not Austin. He was so independent, so focused on setting up on his own, and I admired him for that. At the time, I was more interested in my friends, and parties, and gossip, and a kind-of-distant brother hadn't featured high on my list of priorities.

Another thing I was making up for now.

Austin had retrieved my phone from my flat two days earlier, but it had taken me until now to turn it on. I wasn't sure what was holding me back, but as the screen came to life, I threw it face down on the pillow next to me.

Eventually, I told myself that hiding from my phone wasn't going to achieve anything, so I flipped it over and unlocked my screen.

I scrolled mindlessly through my apps before I admitted to myself that I wanted to see if there was a message from Cassius.

There was more than one.

Much more.

He'd sent me a total of twenty-seven messages, and there were also messages from Winter and Lena. Before I looked at the messages from him, I read through the messages from the girls, which were mostly showing concern and saying to contact them when I felt up to it. After I'd replied to them both, I took a deep breath and opened my message thread with Cassius.

I'd done so well in keeping myself together all this time, but now the tears fell, and I couldn't even say why. Angrily, I swiped them away, grabbing a tissue from the nightstand. This was ridiculous.

When I managed to gather myself, I tapped out a reply to his most recent message, then carefully placed my phone face down again.

Cassius: Are you OK? Hope Austin's looking after you. Text me back when you're ready
Me: Thanks for thinking of me. I'm OK mostly. Almost recovered & enjoying time with my brother

An hour later, after I realised I'd read the same paragraph on my Kindle for the tenth time, I dared to check my phone again.

Cassius: Good. I want to see you. When are you coming home?

I'd had a week to think, and I knew I couldn't do this anymore. It wasn't fair to either of us. It wasn't his fault that I'd fallen in love with him, and I never tried to fool myself into thinking he felt more for me, because I knew he didn't. I'd gone into our arrangement with my eyes wide open, and I knew it had only really ever been about the sex for him. Anything more was just wishful thinking on my part.

Hot tears filled my eyes. I had to do it. I had to end this now before I made things even worse. Still, it took me a long time to type the words, then a long, agonising ten minutes before I forced myself to send my reply.

Me: I'll be home in the next couple of days but I need time to myself. I'm sorry Cass, I have to end our arrangement. It's nothing to do with you I promise

He replied straight away.

Cassius: Can we talk about it? I want to see you. I don't want it to end

A tear landed on my phone screen as I sniffed, my lips trembling. Why did this have to be so hard? Why did doing the right thing have to hurt so much? I knew that he'd be fine, that he'd soon move on, but my heart was breaking as I wilfully pushed away the man I loved.

Me: I can't, I'm sorry. Please give me the space
I need
Cassius: *sad face emoji* I want to see you but if
you need space I can give it to you, as long as you're
OK. Tell me if you change your mind

The tears came in earnest, then.

It was over.

Now I had to find a way to get over Cassius Drummond and move on with my life. Without him in it.

"This is a fucking awkward conversation." Austin half laughed, half groaned.

I couldn't help teasing him a bit as I lay back on the sofa, kicking my legs over the armrest. Running a hand lightly over my ribs, I breathed out steadily, grateful that the pain was no longer there. "How is it awkward? Don't you have conversations about castration very often?"

"Don't say that word to me again," he cautioned. It was now almost three weeks since I'd been back at home, and I was feeling better than I had in a really, really long time. Other than the constant hollow ache inside me, reminding me how much I missed Cassius—that was something I was forcing myself to ignore, because acknowledging it would undo all the progress I'd made. My final year at Alstone College was due to start next week, and I was determined to make the most of it. No more hiding away. I was going to work hard and play hard, but not in the way I'd done previously. I had no desire whatsoever to hook up with any other man, not when my heart belonged to someone else.

Pushing all those thoughts out of my head, I returned

my attention to my brother, adjusting my grip on my phone. "Sorry. So it was some kind of revenge thing because he didn't think that any other woman would want him?"

"Don't you dare feel sorry for him, Jessa. Do I need to remind you what that fucker did to you?"

I sighed. "Believe me, I don't feel sorry for him. I'm... sorry that it all happened, I guess."

His voice softened. "I know. But none of it was your fault." He paused, and I could hear him breathe out heavily before he continued. "It sounds like he took it as a personal offence that you got away from him in the first place. Coupled with his injury—" I could *hear* his wince through the phone, and I couldn't help my smirk, although I did feel bad about it. "—it was enough to set you in his sights. Some people...honestly, Jessa...you'll never really understand their motives. So don't drive yourself mad trying to work out why he did what he did."

"I'm not," I assured him. "In fact—"

My door buzzer sounded loudly. "Hold on, there's someone at the door." I didn't feel any sense of caution anymore, but I still took the time to glance at the small video screen mounted on the wall next to my door that Weston and Lena had installed for me a week earlier. It showed me who was at the entrance door to the building, and as far as everyone else in the building was concerned, who had also received the video upgrade, it was an aspect of security that was well overdue.

Smiling, I hit the button to let my friends in. "I've got to go now. I'll talk to you soon?"

"Will do." Austin was back to his usual businesslike self. Then he added, "Take care, okay?"

A smile curved over my lips. "You too."

When the knock came on my apartment door, I was still

smiling. Winter, Lena, and Kinslee piled in, along with Sophie and Kelly, two other girls from my degree course. I headed into my tiny kitchen to grab the bottles of wine I'd left chilling in the fridge, then returned, placing them down on my coffee table next to the glasses that I'd left there earlier.

"Where shall we put all this?" Kinslee lifted two bags in the air, overflowing with snacks.

"What happened to your dining table?" Lena asked at the same time, eyeing the broken table that I'd propped up against the wall, not having managed to get around to getting rid of it.

"Coffee table?" I suggested to Kinslee, pointedly ignoring Lena's gaze, feeling my cheeks heating.

"Jessa? The dining table?" Lena wasn't letting it go.

"It was your brother, okay?" I buried my face in my hands.

"My broth—ugh!"

Everyone other than Lena fell about laughing as I raised my head. I knew I was still flushed, but I guess it was kind of funny.

"Don't say anything else about it." Lena held a hand in the air. "Seriously."

"I wouldn't dream of it." Giving her an innocent smile, I changed the subject. "Wine, anyone?"

The evening passed in a blur of laughter, conversation about the upcoming semester, and general chat about the people we knew. Nothing malicious, all light-hearted, and I couldn't keep the smile off my face. I could get used to this.

Much, much later, when all the wine was gone and the conversation was winding down, we were sprawled out across the sofa and the floor. One of the *After* movies was playing in the background, and all the girls were deep in discussion about books versus TV and film adaptations. From my position on the floor, leaning my head back against the sofa next to Lena's leg, I stretched my legs out in front of me, tired but happy.

"He misses you." Winter's voice was soft. She was lying on my rug on her stomach, head propped up on her elbows.

My heart beat faster. "Does he?"

She studied me silently, her gaze serious, before she huffed out a breath. "You have to know how he feels about you."

"It was never anything serious with him. Not on his end."

"Do you honestly believe that?"

Lowering my voice, I shifted closer to her. "Yes. Look, I know he enjoyed my company. Enjoyed the, um, sex. But you know what he said to Caiden and Zayde after everything had happened? When he came to my rescue? He said that he would have done the same for anyone, even if it was someone he didn't know."

"He what?" Winter's mouth twisted. "Hang on a minute. He cares about you, Jessa. I... Okay, look, this isn't really my place to say this, but you have to realise. It was him that pushed for getting those camera buzzers installed here. He checks up on you with Austin all the time, and not only that, this evening we're having was his idea. I mean, I was going to suggest getting together anyway, but he came to me with the idea. He worries about you."

I shook my head. This had nothing to do with him feeling any kind of way for me. It was in his nature to care about others, and in my case, it was also the fact that he had a misplaced sense of guilt for everything that had happened to me. "Don't you see? To him, I was a summer fuck buddy. No more or less important than anyone else.

And that's fine, and I've made my peace with it. I knew what I was getting into when I agreed to it in the first place." My voice grew louder, completely unintentionally, as thoughts of him bombarded my mind, one after the other. "I wouldn't change anything about him—he said exactly what I expected he would after he came to my rescue. That's him, isn't it? He would have helped anyone. He cares because he's got the biggest heart, and I love him for it. He's just...well, he's Cassius, y'know?" I finished with a helpless shrug, tears pricking at the back of my eyelids.

It was then that I noticed that the movie had been paused and five pairs of eyes were focused on me.

"So." Lena eventually broke the heavy silence. "You're in love with my brother, huh?"

26

cassius

The day had arrived—the first day of my final year at Alstone College. We'd had our usual "welcome back to Alstone College" party, hosted at our house just two days earlier, and it was then that I knew something was wrong.

Yeah, maybe I knew before then, but coming around to a whole new way of thinking wasn't a quick or easy process for me.

The party, though...

"Who's invited?"

Standing at the kitchen island and staring down at his phone, Cade threw his head up at my question, his brows pulled together. "What do you mean? Everyone's invited. Same as the last two years."

"Everyone?" I kept my voice casual.

"Mate, it's open invite. We always do this." He rolled his eyes in the direction of Z, who just shrugged, content to stay out of it.

"Is..." Fuck, now I had to say it. "Is Jessa invited?"

A smirk stole over Cade's face, and I briefly fantasised about punching him. "Yeah. Jessa's invited. Everyone is. Same as the last two years." I glared at him, and he laughed. "Cass. Never thought I'd see the day. You're so fucked."

"What's that supposed to mean?"

Caiden shook his head, and Z muttered something like "no hope."

Wankers, both of them.

"There'd better be loads of single girls there," I muttered, which just caused them to roll their eyes at me. Again.

"Who are you trying to fool?" The taunting smirk disappeared from Caiden's face, and he took a step closer to me. "You know we don't care if you wanna be with Jessa. She's..." He took a deep breath and gritted his teeth, like he was having to force the words out. "She's...really nice. She's good for you."

Despite myself, I found myself grinning. "Did it hurt to say that?"

He gave me two middle fingers, which was answer enough.

Our not-at-all-awkward discussion was interrupted by the arrival of West, Lena, and Winter carrying armfuls of alcoholic drinks and cups. Perfect timing. After grabbing a huge bag of ice from the freezer, I headed over to the paddling pool I'd blown up earlier and emptied the bag into it. I made another few trips while the others filled it up with cans and bottles, and with us all working together, it was ready in no time. Zayde and Caiden had disappeared a couple of minutes before I heard the music start up, pumping through the house and bringing a huge smile to my face.

I fucking *loved* parties.

An hour later, it was well under way, and maybe I didn't love parties so much.

There was no Jessa.

I drank.

Another hour passed, and still no Jessa.

I drank.

Another hour. I fucking *hated* parties.

I drank.

There were girls. So many girls. I didn't want any of them.

I drank.

Only Jessa.

I drank.

"Did you know Littlefinger gave Jessa a cracked rib?" Lena was suddenly in my face, prodding at my chest.

"What?" I mumbled. *A cracked rib?* No, surely she would have said something.

My chest hurt. "I need to see if she's okay. Where's my phone?"

"Watch it." Her voice was alarmed as I tripped over nothing, flinging my arms out and grabbing onto the nearest solid surface.

The surface shook. "Fucking hell, mate. How much have you had to drink?"

Blinking slowly, I realised that I was holding on to Weston, or was he holding me up...

Fuck. My foot slipped out from under me, and I tightened my grip on West.

"Okay. Outside."

"I've never seen him like this."

"Sit him down. I'll clear the space."

"I'll get some water."

Everything went over my head as I was pushed down onto a hard surface, and then an ice-cold glass was shoved into my hands. "Drink this," a female voice instructed.

I gulped the water, sinking back into the chair. Whispers and murmurs went over my head while I concentrated on the feel of the glass in my hand, condensation dripping down the sides and running over my fingers.

"*Jessa.*"

No one responded, and I realised that I hadn't said the words aloud. The glass slipped from my fingers, and I heard a crash, but it sounded like it came from far away.

The alcohol caught up with me then, and I didn't know anything else.

Cringing, I avoided my hazy memory of the party and concentrated on what was happening right now.

"Our first day of our last year." I stopped in front of the grey stone building that housed the Brunswick lecture hall.

Next to me, Winter sighed. "Yeah. I hope this year we can just concentrate on uni work, but whatever happens, it's going to be hard, isn't it? Everyone says that the final year is the hardest."

Throwing my arm around her shoulders, I dropped a quick kiss on top of her head. "Yeah, babe. But in case you didn't notice, you're part of the Alstone elite. You're the cream of the crop." She raised a brow, so I continued. "You wouldn't be here if you couldn't handle it. You're clever, talented, all that shit, and you know that Cade and West's dad thinks of you as his surrogate daughter or whatever. You've got a guaranteed job at Alstone Holdings after this."

"I know." Her voice was quiet. "I just want to make sure I'm up to it."

"Course you are. You're Winter Huntington, soon to be Cavendish." Giving her a wide smile, I held the building door open for her.

"Soon to be Cavendish. Really. Don't start. With the hints Arlo drops every time we go over there for a meal..." She made an irritated noise, shaking her head, but a smile tugged at her lips. "Why is everyone so impatient? We're still uni students."

"Because you and Cade are goals?" I offered, following her into the lecture hall.

"Maybe." Her gaze turned so fucking soft, and that ache in my chest was back.

I ignored it, sliding into a seat close to the back of the hall next to Winter.

"Last first day of our lectures," she said as she pulled her laptop from her bag and turned it on.

"Last first—"

Every. Single. Thought disappeared from my head as Jessa De Witt strutted into the lecture hall, pausing at the bottom of the stairs like she was allowing everyone to get a good look at her.

Fuck. Me.

She was *so beautiful.*

Her dark hair fell straight and glossy down her back, and her insane curves were poured into tight jeans and a tiny mint green top that reminded me of the bikini she'd worn back at my house.

Her shoulders straightened, and she fixed her gaze on an empty seat a few rows up from the bottom.

It was like the beginning of last year all over again, but the hard expression that she'd had back then was missing from her face. I couldn't even read her expression right now, but I knew her well enough to see the vulnerability that she was trying so desperately to hide.

The realisation crashed over me like some kind of tidal wave, and I couldn't fucking breathe.

I loved her.

How in the actual fucking fuck had I managed to fall in love?

Me?

Fucking hell.

It wasn't even her looks, although that was what had attracted me in the first place, and okay, yeah, her physical appearance made my cock hard. Very, very hard. But there was so much more beneath the surface...all the things about her that made her who she was, and made her important to me.

Now I wanted a relationship. A real, proper relationship.

With Jessa.

I wanted everything with her.

Fucking fuck.

I didn't know how to do this. I'd missed her so much. I guess I should've had a clue from my frequent texts to her brother asking for updates and my borderline stalkerish surveillance of her apartment, but I was so out of my depth here, so used to superficial flirting and sex and...what was I supposed to do?

"Winter!" My voice was panicked as my gaze lifted from Jessa and flicked in her direction.

She didn't even need to say anything. Her blue eyes met mine, full of understanding, and she reached out, rubbing over my arm.

I let my head fall back, pinching my brow. "What am I going to do?"

A slow smile spread across her face. "I'm glad you asked. I have an idea. How comfortable are you talking to Jessa's brother?"

27

jessa

The queue for Sanctuary snaked down the street, and I smiled as Winter and I posed for a selfie, making sure that we had the Sanctuary sign in the background. Despite the club still being fairly new, it was already a venue that people wanted to be seen at. My brother deserved all the success in the world, and I was more than happy to help out however I could by spreading the word and posting photos. Especially now that no one was after me.

My nightmares had more or less disappeared, but I'd been seeing a therapist recommended by Lena, and just having that weekly chat was balancing me like nothing else had.

Things were better, so much better now. But still, I missed Cassius, more than I could ever have imagined.

That saying, "Better to have loved and lost, than to never have loved at all..." it was wrong. If you'd never loved, how would you know what you were missing?

That was another thought that was currently banned from my head.

I focused on my surroundings, smiling at the tall, tattooed bouncer with the shaved head. He waved us in, and I entered the bar area, followed by Winter.

"Want a drink?" Taking a step towards the bar, I was stopped by her hand on my arm.

"Not here. Let's go to the VIP area, shall we?"

"Okay." Turning on my heel, I made my way in the direction of the stairs that led to the mezzanine level. Winter flashed me a smile, darting past me to reach the stairs first. I raised a brow at her unusual behaviour but said nothing, just returning her smile.

When we reached the top of the stairs, I saw Caiden reclined in one of the booths in conversation with my brother and another dark-haired guy.

I came to a stuttering halt. "Oh. I didn't know Cade was going to be here." Shooting Winter a wide-eyed look, I scrambled to amend my words. "I didn't mean...I'm not annoyed that he's here or anything. I just didn't expect—"

Winter laughed, tilting her head to mine. "Don't stress. He's just here to keep me company while you're..."

"While I'm what?" I prompted when she left the sentence unfinished. Her gaze darted to my left, and I turned in time to see a man bounding towards me, all glittery, toned skin and a huge grin on his face.

"While you're with me!" JJ swept me into his arms, placing a loud, smacking kiss on my cheek.

"Hi." I returned his greeting with a pleased smile, then rubbed at the smudge of lipstick I'd left on his cheek. "Sorry, got a bit of lipstick on you."

He gripped my hand, leading me towards the far end of the VIP area. "It wouldn't be the first time. What do you think of my eyeliner? I'm experimenting with upping the glitter count."

I examined him as he batted his lashes at me, showing off the smooth black liner with iridescent silver sparkles shot through it. "I love it. You look hot. Also, I'm jealous of that flick you've managed with the liner. I can never get mine to look that good."

He beamed at me. "Plenty of practice. Anyway, you don't need it. You look..." Coming to a stop in front of the black curtain that led into the lap dance room, he looked me up and down, tapping his lips with a finger. "Effervescent," he said eventually.

"Effervescent? What?"

"Yep. Oh, here we are." Sweeping the curtain aside with a dramatic flourish, he pointed in the direction of the booths. "Take a seat."

The room was dark, even more so than it had been the last time I'd been here, and a low, pulsing beat thrummed through the space, making me want to dance. But curious to see what JJ was up to, I followed his instructions and made my way to the unoccupied booth.

"Are you ready to see some impressive moves?" He spun around in front of me, his entire body shimmering under the lights from head to toe.

"Always," I told him with a smile.

"Good." He drew the thick, heavy curtain around the booth, enclosing us in the space. "Your private dance, my lady."

I reclined back in the booth, watching as he prowled towards me, and then I jumped as he snapped his fingers in my face.

"You need a drink. I'll be back." Then he was ducking out of the booth, closing the curtain behind him. Actually, now he mentioned it, I could do with a drink. It had been a long first week back at uni, settling into the routine of lectures and coursework and attempting not to think about a certain person, and tonight was about having fun with Winter. And Caiden now, I guessed.

Maybe I'd just hang out in here with JJ so I wasn't a third wheel.

My phone buzzed with a message from my dad, reminding me that there was a networking event at Alstone Town Hall on Sunday, hosted by Alstone Holdings, and it would be "nice" if I could attend. In other words, he expected me to be there, which was completely fine but didn't work well with my whole "avoiding Cassius until I got over him" thing. Hopefully, there would be a lot of people in attendance so I could keep my distance. I replied to say that I'd see him there, dropping my phone back into my small handbag just as the curtain rustled, followed by the sound of a bottle clinking on the table.

Placing my bag on the booth seat, I raised my head.

My mouth dropped open.

There was dead silence as we stared at one another.

"You're not JJ," I said stupidly, finally finding my voice.

"Nope." A slow smile spread across Cassius' face, his eyes bright and sparkling with amusement and something else...anticipation, maybe.

I drank him in greedily, not understanding why he was here but knowing that I never wanted him to leave. His body, toned and strong, shone with—was that oil? And the gold shorts...tight didn't even cover it. *Bloody hell*. Very, very few people could make shorts like that look good, but I guess he was one of those few. I mean, they barely covered anything, and all that tanned skin on display was quite honestly frying my brain.

"Don't look at me like that." His voice came out low and

husky, making me shiver, even though he gave me a cheeky grin. "I haven't got room for a boner in these shorts."

"How...what?" I gestured at him.

"Your friend JJ."

Taking a deep breath, I tore my gaze away from his body and back to his face. "What's going on here, Cass?"

"Your private dance." With those words, he stepped closer, leaning down into my space and planting his arms on either side of me. "Remember the rule."

He was so close that I could make out his individual lashes, his breath hitting my lips as he spoke. "No." His body rolled against mine, and my heart raced.

"Touching." Rising up, he straddled me, up on his knees, keeping space between us.

"The." He lowered his hips, and I *ached* for him.

"Dancers." His mouth came down on mine.

It was everything. He consumed me with his kiss, a tsunami of taste and touch and feeling, sweeping me away. I gripped the edges of the seat, the feel of the soft leather grounding me as he kissed me like he'd never kissed me before. Like he'd never get enough.

"Cass," I whispered against his mouth when he paused to take a breath. He stared down at me, breathing hard, his pupils swallowing the blue of his eyes.

"I want you so fucking much." His voice was raw. "Fuck."

"Have me." I leaned up to swipe my tongue across his lips, and he groaned.

"We can't...we're not having sex in your brother's club."

"No one will know," I breathed, arching towards him, my nipples hard and sensitive, brushing against the thin fabric of my dress. The ache between my thighs was impossible to ignore now, my pussy soaked and my clit throbbing.

"What...are your ribs okay?"

Warmth spread through me, his words penetrating the lust that had set my whole body alight. "They're fine."

He breathed out unsteadily, a sigh of relief.

This man was everything. And I needed him now. I'd been fooling myself by thinking I could get over him. Even if this right here was all I got, it would be worth it.

Nipping at his jaw, I murmured my words against his skin, soft and desperate. "I want you so badly, Cass."

My words broke whatever was left of his restraint, and he shifted off me, yanking down the shorts with some difficulty and letting his hard cock spring free. Reaching up for him, I dragged him down onto the booth seat. I straddled him as he hiked up my dress, pushing the damp fabric of my underwear aside, and then slowly sank down onto his thick length.

I was so wet and ready for him, it was an easy glide, and when he was fully inside me, he moaned, his hold on me tightening. "Oh, fuck, Jessa." His head hit the back of the booth as he pulled me down into a messy, desperate kiss.

"I'm not going to last." Already I could feel the orgasm building inside me as I ground myself against him, his cock stretching me in the most delicious way.

"Me neither." His hands gripped my hips, urging me on as he thrust up into me. "So. Fucking. Perfect."

When I came, I felt him shuddering against me, his cock pulsing and filling me up as he found his own release.

He was right. *So fucking perfect.*

After he'd withdrawn from me, I let my body slump forwards, and his arms came up to encircle my body. We stayed like that for a while, wrapped up in each other, and it felt like we were both too afraid to break the silence with the inevitable conversation that had to come.

But eventually, the silence was broken, although not by either of us.

"Care package, courtesy of the dancers' dressing room. And your stuff."

Turning my head, I saw JJ poking his head around the curtain, his whole face alight with humour. He placed a pile of what looked like clothes down on the table next to the forgotten prosecco, then laid a bag on top before disappearing again.

I sighed, climbing off Cassius. "I guess that's our cue." On slightly shaky legs, I made my way over to the table and examined the contents of the bag. "Tissues and baby wipes."

Cassius came to stand next to me. "JJ's a useful bloke to know, huh?"

"It would seem so." We cleaned up in silence, and then Cassius unfolded the pile. Underwear, dark jeans, and a T-shirt. He grinned at my raised brow.

"I had to bring a change of clothes with me. Couldn't go into the main club in those shorts. Not with your brother there." Stuffing said shorts into the bag, he groaned. "Fuck, I think I ripped these when I was taking them off." I laughed as he continued. "Your brother wouldn't have appreciated them as much as you did."

"Or me," came a voice from behind the curtain, and then JJ reappeared. "If you ever want to model them again for me, feel free." He shot Cassius a wink and added, "I'm always available to rub oil into you again, as well."

After he'd also winked at me and grabbed the bag, he disappeared again, and I settled back in the booth, using the tiny mirror in my handbag to fix my hair and smudged makeup. "He rubbed oil into you, did he?"

"Yeah. I wanted to go for the full look." Striking a pose,

he flexed his pecs, and I blew him a kiss, laughing. He pretended to catch the kiss before his face fell. "He wouldn't let me use the glitter, though. Said it would get all over your dress."

His disappointed pout made me smile. "Hmm. Considering that my dress is now covered in your body oil, the glitter probably wouldn't have made much difference."

"Sorry." Sinking down next to me, he bit his lip, glancing at my dress.

"It's okay. It's black, anyway, and the club's dark. I doubt anyone will notice." I hesitantly reached out, sliding my fingers between his, and a small smile appeared on his face.

"This wasn't how it was supposed to happen."

"Oh?" I tilted my head, looking into his eyes.

"I was going to give you a lap dance and impress you with my moves, then I was going to talk to you."

"Well, you definitely impressed me with your moves." My free hand slid onto his thigh, and I gently squeezed. I swallowed hard, gathering my courage, and asked the question. "What did you want to talk to me about?"

His grip on my hand tightened, and he tugged me closer so my body was right up against his. This time when he spoke, his words were soft and serious. "I missed you so much."

"Cass," I whispered.

He stroked his fingers through my hair, brushing it back from my face. "Did-did you miss me?"

There was so much hesitance in his tone, and it took me a minute to formulate a reply. He needed total honesty from me, and I was going to give it. "Yeah, I missed you. I've missed you every single day we've been apart, if you really want to know."

His tongue darted out to lick his lips, and he cleared his throat. "Good. It was the same for me."

"Was it?"

I didn't do a very good job of hiding my surprise, because he sighed heavily and said, "Yes. I was trying to respect your decision and give you space, but I couldn't get you out of my head. Apparently I've been a bit...oblivious about my feelings for you. Or in denial. Whatever, I didn't recognise them for what they were."

"Your feelings for me?" All I could do was repeat his words, breathless with anticipation and hope and longing.

"Yeah." His lips curved upwards. "And I've heard from a very reliable source that you might return those feelings."

"I..." My fingers curled into the denim of his jeans. "I do."

"Okay. Good." He leaned down, brushing his lips against mine, not quite a kiss, but a soft touch that made me melt inside. "I hope you're ready for the epic levels of disappointment this news will bring."

I pulled back, staring at him. "What do you mean?"

His smile widened into the cocky grin that I loved. "When everyone finds out that I'm off the market. It's going to break a lot of hearts."

"I see." I returned his smile. "I'm sure it'll be okay. Plenty more fish in the sea and all that."

"But there's only one Cassius Drummond."

"Yeah." There was a lump in my throat as I closed the distance between us. "You're right. There's only one of you, and you're the only one for me."

"I only want you, Jessa." He captured my lips in a slow, soft kiss. I lost myself in the hot slide of our mouths, his tongue stroking against mine as he deepened the kiss. When he pulled away, he placed one final kiss on my lips.

His gaze dropped to his hands, and I both felt and heard the heaving, unsteady breath that he took before his eyes returned to mine. An unreadable expression crossed his face.

"I'm going to tell you something now. I wasn't going to say it yet, but fuck it. I need to tell you."

I didn't even dare to breathe, my heart pounding so hard that I wouldn't be surprised if it could be heard over the noise of the music. He stared at me, biting his lip, and then he took another deep breath.

"I love you. I know we haven't even properly made this official yet, but, yeah, there it is. I'm in love with you, Jessa De Witt."

A shocked gasp fell from my lips as he spoke the words I hadn't ever imagined he'd say, not in a million years. I'd hoped he might ask me to be his girlfriend, but *this*? I felt the tears filling my eyes as I was hit with a wave of emotion so powerful that I was helpless against it.

"I...I wasn't expecting that. *At all.*" He opened his mouth, but I shook my head, rushing to continue so that I could get the words out before he got the wrong idea. "I love you, Cass. I'm actually stupidly in love with you, and I just wasn't expecting you to feel the same way."

Releasing my hand, he pulled me into his lap, holding me close. "I wouldn't have worn those gold shorts and performed for you if I didn't love you."

I buried my laugh in his chest, loving the feel of him surrounding me with his warmth and strength. "You wouldn't have even needed an excuse to wear those. I know you were dying to."

"I can't confirm or deny that."

"I knew it."

His arms tightened around me, like he never wanted to let me go. "You love me." There was wonder in his tone.

"I do. So much."

"Ready to go back out there and break the news to the others?"

Smiling, I traced a heart pattern over his chest with my finger. "Yes. As long as we avoid mentioning the sex part if my brother's there."

"Yeah, I don't really wanna be subject to his wrath, thanks." He shuddered dramatically against me. "Better find JJ before we go. I owe that man a drink."

"You probably owe him a new pair of shorts, too," I reminded him.

"I do. Might get myself a pair at the same time."

"Why does this not surprise me?"

"So much judgement coming from the girl who reads about turgid members and moist channels."

I punched him in the bicep, and he laughed down at me, his blue eyes bright and his face so happy that I wanted to freeze the moment. How was this my life?

Cassius Drummond *loved* me.

And he owned my heart.

28

jessa

"Thanks for meeting me." Caiden leaned against one of the pillars at the front of Alstone Town Hall, hands in his pockets. "Want to take a walk?"

"Okay." I gave him a cautious glance, and his lips twitched. Barely, but there was the hint of a smile there. A tiny bit of the tension seeped from my body.

He pushed off from the pillar and headed around the side of the building. I fell into step next to him, both of us silent until we reached the gardens behind the town hall. He looked around, then crossed the grass to one of the benches that dotted the space, lining a long, wide avenue with huge trees on either side.

I took a seat next to him with some trepidation. All I knew was what Winter had told me—that he wanted to have a word with me and I had nothing to worry about. Clearly, it had something to do with Cassius, but other than that, I was in the dark. Caiden and I hadn't had the best relationship since Winter had appeared in his life, so whatever he had to say, it probably wasn't anything good.

"Before I say anything..." He paused, picking at a frayed bit on his jeans, his head lowered. "I want you to know that no one forced me to do this. It was my idea." Now he met my eyes, defiance in the stormy depths, as if he was daring me to challenge him.

I didn't know how to reply, so I stayed silent, waiting for him to continue.

Lowering his gaze again, he scuffed the toe of one of his trainers against the ground. "I never thought I'd see the day where Cassius fell for a girl."

"And I bet you didn't think it would be me, either." The words just came out, and I held my breath.

Although he kept his gaze fixed on the ground, a small smile tugged at his lips. "Yeah. I definitely didn't see that coming." He shook his head. "We have a lot of history. All of us do. We've grown up together, and whatever bad shit went down between you and me and Winter this last year, we're going to be in each other's lives for the foreseeable future. Our dads work together—fuck, your dad's socialising with mine and Cass' dad half the time these days."

"I know I already apologised for everything, but—"

Putting his hand up, he shook his head again, finally looking at me. "This isn't about apologies. That's all over as far as I'm concerned, and the past is in the past."

Opening my mouth to reply, I paused when he cleared his throat. "I didn't realise how serious Cass was about you to begin with. We had a talk, and...yeah. A lot of things have become clearer to me."

There was silence for a moment, and I wasn't sure what to say.

"He told me how he can switch off with you, and...fuck." He scrubbed his hand over his face, a frustrated sigh falling from his lips. "All of us have slipped into our roles over the years, I guess. If there's a part of him that feels responsible for always being the one to bring the mood up, then that's something we need to work on. I know I feel pressure to act a certain way sometimes..." Trailing off, he frowned. "Anyway, that's something that me, him, Z, and West need to talk about. The point I'm trying to make here, although I'm clearly fucking it up, is that I know you're here to stay. You're important to Cass, and that means you're important to the rest of us."

I stared at him. This wasn't at all what I'd expected. All I could do was offer him my truth. "I love Cassius. He means everything to me. And I-I really like the rest of you."

He looked at me in silence for a minute, and then he groaned. "This is so fucking awkward. I'm no good with words—just ask Winter."

"I think you're doing alright," I offered softly, earning me another small smile.

"Okay. I guess this is the part where I say 'welcome to the family.'" He affected some deep, unidentifiable accent, which made me laugh.

"What accent was that supposed to be?"

"Not sure, actually. It felt like we were in the mafia, so I was trying to get into the role."

"You are all so weird. What have I got myself into?" I muttered to myself, biting my lip to hide my own smile.

"Yet you're the one reading dodgy porn books."

"For fuck's sake, why does everyone have to keep bringing that up?" There was no hiding my smile anymore.

Caiden stood, grinning, and then he held out his hand to me.

I took it, and he pulled me to my feet.

It felt symbolic.

It felt like a new beginning.

Back inside the town hall a while later, the afternoon networking event was well under way in one of the function rooms. Well-dressed members of the Alstone elite mingled while waiters circulated with trays of champagne and canapés. Caiden disappeared off to talk to his dad, and I looked around, trying to spot Cassius, but I didn't see him. I did, however, see my dad, who made a beeline for me as soon as I caught his eye.

"Jessa. Thanks for coming." He placed a hand lightly on my back, leaning down to kiss my cheek.

"Of course." I smiled. "How's it going?"

"Good, I think. We have a couple of potential orders, big ones at that, which I'll follow up when I'm back in the office tomorrow." He chatted to me about the business for a while, giving me a proud smile every time I chimed in with a suggestion or opinion.

We were interrupted by Arlo Cavendish, Caiden and Weston's dad, who gave me an apologetic smile, steering my dad aside, and I took my chance to escape. I hadn't gone more than three steps when I was pulled back against a familiar, firm body, a tattooed arm sliding around my waist.

"Where are you running off to?" Cassius murmured in my ear, following up his question with a soft kiss to the side of my head.

"I was looking for you, actually." Turning my head, I lifted my face for a kiss.

He smiled against my lips. "Come with me."

With his arm around me, he led me over to where his

parents were standing. Paul and Estella Drummond were part of the Alstone Holdings legacy, and although they were both extremely powerful and influential, there was a warmth and genuineness about them that had always made me feel completely at ease.

"Mum, Dad. Meet Jessa De Witt." Cassius waved his hand in my direction.

"Were you out in the sun too long today, Cassius? We already know Jessa." Paul raised a brow.

"Poor boy. He's sun-addled." Estella shook her head at Paul.

Cassius attempted to glare at them. "I know you know her. I wanted to introduce her officially." He paused dramatically. "As my girlfriend."

Both of them gaped at us, although Estella was quick to hide her surprise, recovering with a genuine smile on her face. "Jessa. How lovely. We must have you both over for dinner soon. Does a day next week work?"

I glanced at Cassius, who gave me a small nod. "That would be great. Thank you, Mrs. Drummond."

She laughed. "No need for formalities. Call me Stella." Stepping closer, she placed a hand on my arm. "Forgive my surprise. It's just that Cassius has never had a girlfriend before, and I was beginning to lose hope of it ever happening."

"He was always too busy sowing his wild oats," Paul interjected with a smirk, and Estella elbowed him in the ribs.

"Thanks for that, Dad," Cassius mumbled.

"Cass has a girlfriend." Lena suddenly appeared at my side, and I didn't miss the huge, exaggerated eye roll Cassius gave her.

"They already know."

Her face fell. "I wanted to be here when you told them."

"Why?" He frowned, and everyone turned to look at her.

She slipped her arm around me, and now I had both her and Cassius hugging me. It was nice. Really nice.

"Because I'm part of this family, too, and Jessa's my friend. She might've needed me for moral support."

"We're not that scary, are we?" Paul laughed.

"You're not, but have you met your son? I was worried he'd embarrass Jessa or scare her away."

Paul nodded. "Fair point. But I think we can all agree that everything went well. Cass has exceptional taste. Takes after his dad, of course." He shot me a tiny wink. "Now, if you'll excuse me, I need to catch Thomas before he leaves." Lifting a hand to catch the attention of someone behind me, he stepped aside, and when Lena moved away from me to speak to Estella, Cassius leaned down to kiss my cheek.

"Was that okay?" His voice was soft in my ear.

"Yeah." I nodded, turning to press a kiss to his jaw. "Of course it was."

"Good."

Someone tapped him on the shoulder, and we both turned to see Caiden standing with Zayde and Weston. "Are you ready to leave?"

"Yeah." Cassius' voice was relieved. "I've done enough networking for one afternoon."

"I'd done enough in the first ten minutes of being here." Caiden shrugged at him, then turned to me, his gaze warm and open. "Jessa? Coming home with us?"

I stared at him, a smile slowly spreading across my face, which grew wider when Zayde spoke up, looking directly at me. He only said one word, but it was enough, especially when I saw his lips tilt up at the corners. "Come."

"Yeah, come on. I wanna show you an idea I had for those buzzer cameras." West threw me a grin as he slung his arm over Caiden's shoulder.

Cassius pulled me into him, ducking his head, and I could feel his smile against my neck.

What else could I say?

"Okay."

EPILOGUE 1

jessa

ONE WEEK LATER

Cassius threw his phone down on the sofa with a grin as I settled into place next to him after carefully placing the mug of tea I'd made him down on the coffee table. "Your brother always has the best memes."

"*My* brother? Austin? Sending memes?"

"Yep."

"How is it that I didn't know this? And also, why do you talk to my brother more than I do?"

He tugged me into his lap. "No one can resist my charms, not even Austin."

"Okay, I suppose that's true." I kissed the side of his throat. "Mmm. You smell nice." Breathing in, I trailed my nose up his neck, noticing the hitch in his breath as he tilted his head.

"I'll never get enough of you." His hand slid up my thigh.

"Did you forget we were here?"

I jerked away from Cassius to see Weston grinning at me from the armchair, with Lena stretched out on the floor and leaning back on his legs, tapping at her phone screen.

"No, I didn't forget." Shooting him a smile, I watched in satisfaction as he shook his head.

"You've been spending too much time with Cass. He's rubbing off on you."

"I'd like to rub one off on you right now," Cassius murmured in my ear, and I reached up to cover his mouth. He licked my palm, and I made a noise of disgust, yanking my hand away.

"Do you have to?"

"Yep." His voice was unrepentant.

"Did I tell you about the time Cass licked my ear, right when we were in the middle of a serious mission?" West leaned forwards in his seat, his fingers sliding through Lena's hair. "We'd managed to infiltrate this illegal dog-fight—"

"Infiltrate? You make us sound like secret spies," Cassius interrupted him.

He rolled his eyes. "Spies are secret by nature. You can't be a secret spy."

"You can."

"You can't."

"You can."

"You can't."

"Okay, is someone going to tell me about this illegal dog-fight?" I cut in before the conversation could get out of hand. I noticed Lena smirking from behind her phone screen, so I stretched out my legs and nudged her calf with my toe. If I had to be involved in this conversation, then she did, too.

She placed her phone down and gave me her full attention. "Yeah. It was your ex-best friend, Portia, who gave me the breakthrough in the end."

"*Portia*? What?"

"Technically, it was James Granville who identified her, but Portia was instrumental in the whole thing." Pulling up her legs, she wrapped her arms around her knees. "Ready for a story? It all started when I found out about these illegal dog-fights that were taking place in Alstone..."

As she spoke, I curled into Cassius, soaking up his warmth and listening to the three of them weave a story that I wouldn't have believed if they hadn't been the ones to tell it. The whole time they talked, Cassius had his hand on me, stroking my hair, my leg, my sides. Constantly reminding me that he was here.

I couldn't ever remember being so content.

A while later, when it had grown dark outside and I was starting to feel sleepy, Zayde wandered in to join us, followed closely by Winter and Caiden. They all sprawled around in the large lounge, relaxed, the conversation low and easy.

"Austin gave me the big-brother talk." Cassius suddenly broke the comfortable silence we'd both fallen into.

"He what?" I twisted my head to stare up at my boyfriend.

"Yeah, you know. The 'don't hurt my sister or I'll be forced to tie concrete blocks to your ankles and throw you into the River Thames' talk."

"He did not say that." I narrowed my eyes at him.

Cassius widened his eyes, full of attempted innocence, but I could read him too well. I saw the humour sparkling in them as he met my gaze. "Maybe I was paraphrasing."

"Misinterpreting, more like."

"Cass gave me that talk, too," Weston said, and it was

then that I realised that everyone else had also fallen silent and was listening to our conversation. "He said he'd cut my balls off if I hurt Lena."

"You keep saying you're a lover, not a fighter, but you have such violent tendencies, Cass." Winter shook her head in mock disappointment.

"Wait, no. I said Z would cut his balls off," Cassius protested.

"So it was *you* who started that rumour? As if poor Zayde doesn't have enough to deal with already, what with his serial killer stare and everything." Winter darted a look at Zayde, who was clearly unimpressed. To my surprise, she untangled herself from Caiden and threw herself into his arms. "You know I don't mean it."

Even more surprising, he hugged her back.

"The words 'poor' and 'Zayde' don't belong together in a sentence. He's like the mysterious bad boy, with all that and his motorbike. He could probably have more girls than any of us ever had, if he could be bothered." Cassius pointed at Zayde as he said "that," and I assumed he meant his many tattoos and piercings and his general "keep away" vibes that he threw out.

Zayde gave Caiden a casual shrug, and I scrutinised him. Yeah, there was an appeal to him, if you liked that sort of thing, but as for me, my type consisted of one man only, and he was currently trailing kisses down the side of my face.

I smiled, turning my head up to capture his lips.

The conversation turned to bikes, and then to cars, and then something about revs and torque, by which point I'd slyly opened my Kindle app on my phone and begun to read the fourth instalment in my elf fantasy series, keeping my screen tilted away from the others.

"His weeping mushroom head stared up at her, angry and purple, seemingly throbbing with delicious anticipation. As she spread her legs, exposing the delicate moist petals of her flower—"

"*Cassius*!" I buried my head in the sofa cushions to the sound of everyone's laughter.

Again.

EPILOGUE 2

cassius

ONE MONTH LATER

"Want to make a bet?" I eyed my girlfriend as she lay spread out on my bed completely naked, like some kind of tempting buffet I wanted to feast on.

"What kind of bet?" Jessa's voice was breathy, her pupils huge, and a glance between her legs told me she was already wet and ready for me. Just the way I liked her.

"Remember, don't move your hands."

She nodded, her arms stretched above her head, her fingers just touching the headboard. I hadn't restrained her. I couldn't bring myself to, the thought of when I'd found her bound and helpless still too recent in my mind. In actual fact, I was 90 percent sure she would be all for me tying her up because she trusted me, but I guess that image of her inside my head would take a while to go away.

"What kind of bet?" she said again, and I pushed all the negative thoughts from my mind.

"A bet on how many letters of the alphabet it'll take to

make you come." Leaning forwards, my arms on either side of her, I placed open-mouthed kisses across her collarbone.

"What?" The word came out on a moan. Her back arched as I lowered my head to take one of her nipples into my mouth, and my cock jerked against the sheets.

Fuck. I'd always thought that I wanted variety, but sex with the girl I loved was incomparable. Nothing even came close.

"Alphabet, baby." Releasing her nipple, I turned my attention to the other one, her shuddering breaths going straight to my hard dick. But this wasn't about me, so I ignored my neglected cock for now.

Kissing and licking my way down her body, I stopped right above where she wanted me, blowing a breath over her wetness. "Ready?" She shuddered, raising her head to stare down at me, her cheeks flushed and her full lips red from where she'd been biting them in an attempt to stay quiet.

"Yes," she panted, losing the battle to keep her arms above her head, her hand coming down and gripping a handful of my hair. "*Please*. Just..."

I got the hint.

"No more talking. But..." I slid my finger between her legs, coating it in her arousal before I pushed it inside.

The moan that fell from her lips was so erotic that my dick fucking throbbed.

I reminded myself again that this wasn't about me. This was all about the girl I loved.

"How many letters?" I pushed another finger inside, curling it.

She gasped. "Uh. Fourteen."

"Do you know what you're betting?" Raising my head, I

looked into her eyes, all unfocused and glassy. Yeah, she had no idea.

"N-no," she managed as I lowered my head, my tongue dragging across her clit in one slow, smooth movement. Another shuddering gasp escaped her at the first touch of my tongue.

"Get ready." Removing my fingers, I licked a long line down her soaked pussy, then brought my hand back down, easing two fingers back inside her. My mouth closed over her clit, and I began.

By the time my tongue got to *D*, she was clamping her thighs on either side of my head.

As I reached *H*, she was writhing on the bed, sexy as fuck moans falling from her mouth.

When I hit *L*, she fell apart, her whole body shaking against me as she called out my name over and over again.

"Cass. Come here." Her rasped words, combined with the tug on my hair, had me moving up her body to rest my head next to hers, my arms automatically wrapping around her.

I held her tightly, and it was weirdly easy to ignore my erection.

"I love you." The words came out so easily.

"I love you, too." She placed a soft kiss to my chest. "Did I win the bet?"

"No, sorry, baby. You guessed fourteen, and it was twelve letters."

"But you didn't bet against me," she pointed out, her lips smiling against my skin as she tracked more kisses across my chest.

"Oh, yeah."

My brain went more or less offline as her hand came down to wrap around my cock. Then, when she slid down the bed and her mouth replaced her hand, there was no way I could think anymore.

Much, much later, when we'd both recovered and cleaned up, she curled up against me in her favourite position with her head on my chest and her arm slung across me, while I lay on my back with my arm curled around her.

"I'll never get enough of you," I murmured into her hair.

"Mmm. Same," she said, all soft and sleepy, and it tugged at something inside me. I loved this woman so much.

"Good." My arms tightened around her. "You need to get some sleep. Big day tomorrow."

"Why?" Her voice had suddenly lost its sleepy tone.

"You'll have to wait and see. Sleep now."

Stroking my hands over her back, I thought of the surprise that waited on the driveway. Her Mercedes, but not...thanks to a bit of help from my boys.

Instead of its original grey, its colour now matched the other cars parked outside.

A perfectly flawless matte black.

I listened to Jessa's soft breaths evening out as she drifted into sleep, and I smiled.

What did I say? All the best love stories start with an epic blowjob.

Mine did.

THE END

ACKNOWLEDGMENTS

First of all, thank you to everyone that has read The Four series! Thank you for taking a chance on Cassius and Jessa's story, and I hope you loved it!

To Claudia, for convincing me that I had to stay true to Cassius and write his story with Jessa, even though almost everyone else thought it was insane! I love you! I'm so thankful for your support and encouragement.

Thank you to to Jenny, Megan, Jen, and Ashley, for your endless support and alpha/beta feedback. Jenny and Jen— you both work so hard and I'm so grateful for everything you do! Love you guys.

Sandra, Rumi, and Sid—dream team! Thank you for getting this story into shape, and for not complaining (much) about my liberal use of commas.

Thanks to all the team at Wildfire, my awesome street team and ARC team, and to all the bloggers who helped to promote this book.

To the readers, bloggers, bookstagrammers, and everyone who has shared, read, enjoyed the world of The Four, you are amazing!

A huge thank you to my Facebook group Becca's Book Bar for voting on a middle name for Cassius, and to Marissa Rash for coming up with the final choice! And I have to give a special mention to the two very kind people who helped me out with the Russian pronunciations in this book.

Lastly, I have to thank my husband, who will never read these words, but you support me in more ways than you know.

Becca xoxo

ALSO BY BECCA STEELE

LSU Series

Blindsided (M/M)

The Four Series

The Lies We Tell

The Secrets We Hide

The Havoc We Wreak

*A Cavendish Christmas (free short story)**

The Fight In Us

The Bonds We Break

Alstone High Standalones

Trick Me Twice

Cross the Line (M/M)

*In a Week (free short story)**

Savage Rivals (M/M)

Boneyard Kings Series (with C. Lymari)

Merciless Kings (RH)

Vicious Queen (RH)

Ruthless Kingdom (RH)

Other Standalones

*Mayhem (a Four series spinoff)**

Heatwave (a summer short story)*

London Players Series

The Offer

London Suits Series

The Deal

The Truce

The Wish (a festive short story)*

Box Sets

Caiden & Winter trilogy

*all free short stories and bonus scenes are available from https:// authorbeccasteele.com

**Key - M/M = Male/Male (gay) romance

RH = Reverse Harem (one woman & 3+ men) romance

ABOUT THE AUTHOR

Becca Steele is a USA Today and Wall Street Journal bestselling romance author. She currently lives in the south of England with a whole horde of characters that reside inside her head.

When she's not writing, you can find her reading or watching Netflix, usually with a glass of wine in hand. Failing that, she'll be online hunting for memes, or wasting time making her 500th Spotify playlist.

Join Becca's Facebook reader group Becca's Book Bar, sign up to her mailing list, or find her via the following links:

facebook.com/authorbeccasteele
instagram.com/authorbeccasteele
bookbub.com/profile/becca-steele
goodreads.com/authorbeccasteele

Made in the USA
Middletown, DE
06 October 2024